IN THE
FRAME

IN THE FRAME

PAT SULLIVAN

IGUANA

Copyright © 2025 Pat Sullivan
Published by Iguana Books
720 Bathurst Street
Toronto, ON M5S 2R4

This book is a work of fiction. Names, characters, places, and events are products of the author's imagination or are used fictitiously. Any resemblance to actual events or places or persons, living or dead, is entirely coincidental.

Publisher: Cheryl Hawley
Front cover design: Jonathan Relph

ISBN 978-1-77180-733-3 (paperback)
ISBN 978-1-77180-732-6 (epub)

This is an original print edition of *In the Frame*.

For my parents, who laughed together

THURSDAY

CHAPTER 1
GEORGE

George Caldwell, director of the Toronto Art Gallery, was in a bad mood. He flung himself back in his black leather chair and fixated on the three photographs hanging on the wall to his right. One image showed him clasping the hand of the Minister of Culture as she presented a cheque. In the next, he looked earnestly at a leading Canadian art collector and philanthropist. In the third, he grinned with a famous rock star — a painter on the side — whom the marketing department had cajoled into visiting the gallery. Usually, these mementos of his proudest moments lifted his spirits, but this morning, they weren't enough. He glared at today's *Toronto Tribune*, the source of his anger, but couldn't stop himself from reading the offending article again.

TAG21 Campaign Launches Tomorrow

Simon Kinsella

Arts Reporter

Tomorrow night marks a milestone in the history of the Toronto Art Gallery (TAG) as it launches a fundraising campaign for a new wing, to be completed in the year

2000. One hundred of the city's top philanthropists have paid a thousand dollars each to be wined and dined by the gallery's executive and board members, who hope to convince them to pledge substantial amounts of money to the two-year project, which is estimated to cost $150 million.

Director George Caldwell, defending the need for the expansion, says, "We have one of the best collections of Canadian, European, and contemporary art in Canada. Thanks to the support of our donors and public funders, it is growing, as is our ability to attract the top travelling exhibitions. We need new galleries to display more of these stellar works for the benefit of our public. We hope that Torontonians will support our building campaign so in two years we can all enjoy an enhanced gallery."

According to a media release, the campaign's slogan, TAG21, embodies the gallery's commitment to embracing the new century.

The Toronto Art Gallery opened in 1930, eight years after the civic-minded Miss Susannah Littlewood donated her Victorian home and property, at Lauriston and Queen streets, to display her collection of European and early Canadian paintings and sculpture. At the time, the museum comprised only five galleries around the impressive Littlewood Court, but since then TAG has witnessed two major expansions. The first, in 1962, saw the construction of additional exhibition spaces, a restaurant, and a studio for art classes. The next renovation, in 1980, brought it to its present state, an architecturally diverse complex that has taken over most of Miss Littlewood's beloved estate to make room for galleries, offices, a conservation lab, and a shop. The proposed wing will extend into one of the few remaining undeveloped corners of the estate: a forty-metre strip of garden at the back.

Mr. Caldwell, who has been at the helm of the gallery for three years, presided over the tricky process of renaming the institution, once known as the Susannah Littlewood Art Gallery (SLAG). According to Miss Littlewood's descendants and other arts enthusiasts, the unfortunate acronym called forth associations that did not suit the founder's image or the gallery's. Mr. Caldwell said of the rebrand, "While we will always honour our origins, the current name and its shorter handle, TAG, convey a more dynamic message for the approaching 21st century."

A less successful example of Mr. Caldwell's leadership is his decision last year to present *Monet's Moments: Impressionist Paintings*, a dated show from France. The exhibition failed to attract the predicted attendance and revenue, resulting in a net loss for the gallery.

Increasing attendance and funding are the twin challenges of today's cultural institutions, so it remains to be seen whether tonight's gala reception and dinner, concocted to entice the cream of Toronto's cultural elite, will be enough to fund Mr. Caldwell's great hopes for TAG's launch into the future.

Damned hack! thought George. "Dated show from France?" What the fuck did Kinsella know about art? George had to concede that the rest of the article was accurate, even tending toward positive, but it irked him that Kinsella had to remind the *Tribune*'s readers of his failure. *Monet's Moments* was in the past, and tomorrow was all about the future.

George stroked the Harvard MBA ring he wore on his right little finger, his habit when stressed. That, and his Rolex watch, a gift from his parents when he became director, helped affirm the determination he felt his position required. At forty-six, he wore his salt-and-pepper hair short, which suited his deep-set brown eyes and square chin. Most of his suits came from Harry Rosen — tailored to his six-foot frame, classic rather than trendy. He particularly liked the charcoal wool one he wore with a light gray shirt today. It completed the look of professionalism he sought to convey.

The stroking failed to evoke its usual magic, so George strode to another source of comfort — the small-scale model of the Toronto Art Gallery expansion, resplendent on a table across his office. A larger-scale model would be on view at the gala, along with architectural renderings of the new spaces. As if an alchemist had imbued the balsa wood and foamcore with fortifying properties, George seemed to inhale confidence when he bent his tall frame to study it. He forgot Kinsella's stinging jibes as he looked adoringly at the imposing main entrance on the east facade, then focused on the west side, where a rectangular shape projecting from the existing sculpture hall indicated the new wing. It would house more European galleries on the ground floor and more contemporary ones on the second level. The wing occupied a large portion of the remaining patch of Miss Littlewood's estate, which had always appeared empty to him, in spite of visitors' enjoyment of the gardens and benches. He knew that Toronto's philanthropic elite would leap at the chance to make his vision become a reality.

George's reverie was interrupted by a knock on his door. His assistant ushered in Victor Drake, chairman of the board of trustees. George suppressed a sigh as he turned to face the man with whom he'd spent so much time over the past few months, discussing the new wing, the gala, and the fundraising campaign.

A few inches shorter than the director, and fifteen years older, Victor had bushy-browed beady eyes set in a fleshy face. Befitting his role as CEO of Drake Properties, he conveyed an air of command, too commanding for George at times, although he valued his chairman's support. The gala attendees would hear more about that support tomorrow night, when Victor would announce the donation of his beloved collection of eighteenth- and nineteenth-century British horse paintings to TAG. George didn't care if connoisseurs considered them the worst or the best hunting scenes ever produced. What mattered was Victor's second announcement: a gift of ten million dollars to kick off the fundraising campaign. Cultivating the chairman's philanthropy required perseverance, but George felt such a bountiful harvest made his hours of patient tilling worth it.

As they sat, Victor said, "Let's get this thing built." Waving a thickset arm toward the model, he nearly swatted George's assistant as she returned with a tray of coffee. "Oops, sorry, dear." When she shut the door, his smile vanished as he turned back to George and snapped, "Get some people into your gallery."

Ours when it's going well, mine when it's a problem, thought George. It wasn't the first time that he ignored the chairman's selective use of pronouns regarding their roles at the gallery. George prided himself on his handling of large egos, otherwise known as donor relations. He knew the attendance figures had increased recently, far exceeding the deserted level that Victor's phrase seemed to suggest.

"More people might be a better way of putting it. With the new wing, the enhanced entrance, and reconfigured education spaces, our numbers will definitely increase. I like to think that our repeat patrons will become even more loyal, while we'll attract a more diverse range of newcomers too."

"Yeah, I know all that. You don't have to give me the pitch, George. I know we've checked all the boxes to please the government funders, but doesn't it bug you that the museum consistently outranks TAG in attendance?"

"Nobody can compete with dinosaurs, Victor," said George. He suspected that Victor knew a business rival on the board of the Museum of Ontario who taunted him with their statistics. Nonetheless, he did his best to put the chairman at ease. "We've projected our numbers based on other art galleries our size, and we'll meet them."

"And you still think TAG21 is going to open up pockets?" When Victor became chair of the campaign, he eagerly suggested names for it, such as "Breed the Best!" or "Back a Winner!" But the development staff, not sharing his love of horses, failed to see how such equine associations would steer money their way, so George had diplomatically convinced Victor that a future-embracing name would work better. Victor's skepticism rankled.

"We've been over this. The development department's already had favourable reaction to the name. I'm counting on your support for it at the gala."

"Sure. Let's hope it brings in the money. You'll need it to attract bigger shows with a higher profile. You don't need another *Manet's Moments* thing."

It was Monet's Moments, *you idiot.* George stifled both his irritation at Victor's careless approach to exhibition titles and the framing of another sore spot as his sole decision. Last year, he had assumed that the borrowed French show's success would justify his bumping another project from the temporary exhibition galleries. Victor had encouraged him.

"Monet's the big guy, right? And Impressionism is a sure bet? Hit 'em with the two best sales pitches right in the name. Should be a blockbuster!"

Victor's vocabulary, George thought, often owed more to the retail world of his shopping mall empire than the upper-crust milieu where he purchased his hunting pictures. But his chairman's enthusiasm for the title was not shared by the art-loving public. Determined to deflect all negative situations, he thought he had presented a positive slant in his report to the board, so Victor's comment annoyed him.

"*Monet's Moments*," corrected George. "But we've put that behind us, right, Victor?"

"Monet, right. Who needs second-rate paintings from some godforsaken French museum that needs to do some renovations? We'll be on the map for the big shows once the new wing opens," said Victor. "By the way, I want to move some of my paintings around the house. Can you send over one of your art handlers to take care of it?"

George sipped his coffee. Even if he was inclined to cater to any and all requests from his board members, for such personal service from the gallery's expert staff, he knew he'd face an outcry from the union steward and the exhibitions head, who would resent sparing any technicians. And George agreed with them. He had to keep Victor happy, but there were limits, which Victor was pushing in other ways too. He sighed inwardly and remembered the inspirational phrase he'd learned in a donor relations seminar — "the gift that keeps on giving." With Victor, he sometimes wanted to amend it to "the gift that keeps on taking."

George fended off Victor's request for help with a referral to a dealer who hired out his handler for a fee. The chairman returned to another favourite topic.

"I still think that second appraisal's a bloody nuisance. You've got that paperwork on Hathaway? He's the one I want to do it. Don't bother asking your curator to find someone."

George bit his tongue. Victor's aversion to paying taxes hummed like an annoying undertone in all of their more positive discussions of the new wing, the gala, and the campaign. He wanted his collection appraised as highly as possible so as to receive the best possible tax credit when he donated it. He had blithely assured George that the British dealer from whom he had purchased most of the works, Lionel Hathaway, was the man to do it. George thought otherwise, knowing Hathaway's shady reputation, but was saved from arguing with Victor by another knock on the door.

"Roger's here. He'd like a minute," said his assistant.

"That's okay," said George with relief. "Roger, just the man." TAG's chief curator, Roger Laplante, entered the room but stopped when he saw Victor.

"Uh, thank you, George. Hello, Victor. George, I'm sorry to interrupt, but I do need this document signed today." He passed a piece of paper across the desk.

"No problem, Roger. Take a seat." George slid the paper toward him and reached for his engraved pen, but kept his eyes on the new arrival. "We were just talking about Victor's donation."

"Ah," said Roger, glancing at Victor with a stiff smile. George knew that Roger, who was also the curator of European art, had spent hours with Victor, listening to his ideas for how his collection should be displayed in the new wing. The curator had won a small victory by convincing Victor that a rotunda in the middle of the proposed European galleries would highlight his horse paintings beautifully, thus freeing up other spacious rooms for works, like their recent Degas acquisition, that Roger thought much more worthy of his attention.

"Can you remind us why we need to get two appraisals for Victor's collection?" George saw a slight frown appear on the curator's face. This point had been well covered in meetings and memos, so he understood Roger's puzzlement as to why he asked again. He trusted that Roger knew the chairman well enough to run with it.

"Your collection's worth more than fifty thousand dollars, Victor. If you want to get the highest possible tax credit, we have to provide two appraisals. I'm afraid the government agency requires that for any large donation, and we have to comply." Roger gave one of his French-Canadian shrugs. "A small price to pay for your magnificent generosity."

Good touch, thought George as he watched Victor's expression change from irritation to pride. It didn't last.

"Hmph. Damned red tape. It's just a make-work project for nosy bureaucrats," grumbled Victor.

"Not at all," said Roger. "We have a list of very competent appraisers we provide to all our donors and the process works extremely well." Roger turned to George with a look that signalled he wanted to escape. George scanned the short document and signed it.

"Thanks, Roger."

"See you tomorrow night, Victor. We're all looking forward to your speech."

The chairman gave Roger a clipped smile. As the chief curator shut the door, George couldn't help thinking that Victor's speech would allow him to emulate the hunters in his paintings by blowing his own horn. George wished that Victor focused on that imminent gratifying moment instead of glaring at him now.

"I still want Hathaway to do it if it's so important. I'll contact him."

"No, Victor. Leave it to us. Now, are you sure of the schedule for tomorrow? Anything you want to go over?" George knew that the prospect of Victor's rise in the ranks of Toronto's philanthropic elite usually deflected him from his tax obsession. To his relief, it worked again. After they reviewed the schedule for what George hoped was the last time, Victor left.

Needing more solace, George walked over to the model again, wincing as his knee twinged, an injury from a squash game last night. It had better not trouble him tomorrow. He wanted to look like the master of his domain — a sizable one comprising twenty-one thousand works of art, twenty-five galleries, and 178 full- and part-time employees. His was a kingdom that included the conservators in the north-facing laboratory who cleaned the art and the workers in plant services who cleaned the washrooms. He oversaw the curators who acquired new works and the technicians and lighting designers who installed and lit them, the marketing and communications department who told the world about the art and the educators and volunteers who helped visitors to engage with it. Every specialized role contributed to his empire, an empire that would become even larger once the new wing became reality.

George congratulated himself again on changing the gallery's name. He'd been prescient. Since January, Metropolitan Toronto had amalgamated, ditching the old structure of six civic governments in favour of one unified mega-city, a formation fit for the twenty-first century. Just as the city had streamlined its name, so had the gallery. TAG was a brand more appealing to donors, a bold, attractive, positive message to convey the value of a new wing. He felt the expansion, like the new name, would cement his legacy of visionary leadership and attract more visitors, which would in turn increase the gallery's donations and government grants.

He bent to rub his knee, studying the model as he did so. He felt as if the balsa wood structure emitted an inner light, beckoning him to approach in awed contemplation. He'd often heard his curators talk about the aura surrounding original works of art, some intangible quality that evaded reproduction. It called out to people, enticing them to enter galleries and stand in front of a given painting, sculpture, print, photograph, or installation for the sole purpose of absorbing its physical reality. For George, the model, even though it embodied a future potential rather than a present actuality, radiated a similar glow.

Reluctantly, he turned back to his desk. Tomorrow, his dream would start to materialize. In the meantime, despite Simon Kinsella's misgivings and Victor Drake's demands, he had a gallery to run.

CHAPTER 2
AMANDA

In her office one floor below George's, Amanda Bharti attacked the endless demands faced by a curator of contemporary art: emails from artists seeking exhibitions, notices of new shows from dealers, calls from the exhibitions department about a technical glitch in an electronic work. A media release announcing a new acquisition waited for her approval. An ever-growing pile of folders lay on her desk and partially-read art magazines covered her credenza. Amanda sent her tenth email of the morning and stretched, then reached for her cooling cup of green tea.

She stroked one of her gold hoop earrings. They enhanced her dark hair and eyes and went well with her ochre-brown wool suit and top. Five foot seven and slim, Amanda wore designer clothes well, and she looked forward to wearing a new dress at tomorrow's gala.

The new wing held as much importance for Amanda as it did for George and Victor. She was eager to install recently acquired works in the new galleries in two years' time, works that languished in the storage vaults now due to lack of room. George had emphasized that he and Victor expected the campaign to launch brilliantly, garnering many pledges. All the curators knew they had to play their parts, to mingle with the well-heeled patrons and talk up the expansion, especially during dinner, when they would sit with potential donors particularly interested in their areas of expertise. She hoped that the gleaming model, the architectural renderings, and the rousing speeches would impel the wealthy attendees to stoke the building campaign. TAG needed more exhibition space, not to mention expanded storage vaults and interior renovations. She doubted that the director's drive to make the new wing a reality owed much to her, but she wanted the contemporary galleries to be the best in Canada.

She sighed and opened a folder on her computer. Damn. Another bloody label to rewrite. She gritted her teeth and started to read it, determined to deal with this annoying task before her meeting with George at eleven.

The folder contained label text for a new acquisition, written by Samantha, the interpretive planner in education who worked with the contemporary department. Amanda would rather just write the labels herself, but George had initiated a new system: all labels would be written by the interpretive planners. Apparently, they possessed a magic hold on accessibility that no mere curator could touch, so she and her colleagues had to content themselves with writing catalogues. Curators still had the right to read the planners' texts. The decision on who had final say swung about like a pendulum, depending on personalities. Amanda usually let her assistant take her comments back to Samantha and battle it out until they achieved consensus, a result magically contrived by the exhibitions head's haranguing them to meet the copy deadline.

But she felt more proprietary about this label, which described a fictional archive of Chile's political upheavals by an important new artist named Pedro Havilio. Proud of the fact that she'd beaten the National Gallery in acquiring the piece, she knew that a donor who had contributed to the purchase eagerly awaited its display. But Samantha's label was inadequate. Why did education always have to dumb down her content? Amanda read it again:

> Pedro Havilio's *Archive* is a fictional collection of documents and photographs related to Chile's turbulent history during the dictatorship that ruled his country from

> 1973 to 1990. Thousands of people disappeared during this period, while many others fled into exile. Havilio imaginatively reconstructs their stories and asks us to consider the difficulty of searching for truth, when so much has been lost.

Amanda couldn't argue with the first sentence. She supposed it could stay. But not the next two. She quickly wrote a replacement:

> Thousands of citizens disappeared under mysterious circumstances during this fraught period, while a diaspora of traumatized refugees and scarred witnesses endured exile. In producing — amassing, collecting — these proto-real, hyper-actual visual and textual documents, Havilio radically ruptures the spatial-temporal action of memory. His proposition, in its globality, galvanizes the dialectic of veracity and depletion.

There! Anyone who knew anything about art would get so much more out of that. She emailed the amended label to Samantha and turned her attention to a more pleasant project. Opening a folder labelled "Expansion," she spread out the photocopies of architectural plans and drawings. Her favourite one showed the plan of the foyer in the new wing, an area that had started out as a passageway between the existing sculpture hall and the entrance to the future spaces. But Amanda had seen its potential to hold an enormous sculpture, something much larger than any of her current rooms could accommodate, and persuaded George to increase the floor plan. With a two-storey height, a mezzanine on the second floor, and visibility through glass walls and doors, the space called out for an original commissioned work unlike anything yet seen in Toronto. And she was zeroing in on the artist to provide it.

Over the past two years, she had come to know Simone Brodeur, an inventive sculptor with several public commissions in major Canadian cities. Simone's exhibition *Gestes* was currently on view at TAG. A complex production involving four cameras and a computerized projection, it represented a culmination of her video work. Simone's current exploration of new materials — aluminum and lights — intrigued Amanda. The two-storey foyer of the new wing could easily accommodate a huge, suspended piece, and she thought that Simone could produce the kind of stunning creation she wanted. It wouldn't hurt her career to support another Canadian woman artist, either; her resume, male-dominated before her move to Toronto from Vancouver, had shifted in its gender balance through her subsequent shows and acquisitions. The award-winning Simone Brodeur would polish her reputation and help her move to new challenges, like a prestigious American gallery. Although it was early days, with the fundraising campaign just launching tomorrow, Amanda felt so confident that she had mentioned the possible commission to Simone, who, not surprisingly, welcomed it.

It was almost eleven, so she hurried down the corridor to the stairwell and dashed up one flight, wondering what George could possibly want with her today. As she strode toward his office, she saw Victor Drake waiting by the elevator. She assumed he'd been in to see the director, no doubt raking over the details of the gala yet again. Victor didn't belong to Amanda's carefully nurtured circle of donors, but she knew she had to respect his dual positions as chair of the board and of the TAG21 campaign. She never knew when she might need him sometime.

"Hello, Victor. How nice to see you! I bet you're looking forward to tomorrow night."

She was taken aback by Victor's surly expression as he looked up from contemplating the elevator buttons. Then his broad face crimped into a perfunctory smile.

"Hi, Amanda. Yes. You should be too. I hope you've got a load of deep-pocketed pals ready to cough up." He stepped into the elevator and the doors shut as Amanda stuttered "Bye."

That was blunt, even for Victor. She wondered if his resolve to build the new wing surpassed the director's, given that his British horse paintings — scenes of wealthy eighteenth-century landowners gathered with their hounds before a fox hunt, or noble steeds silhouetted against green meadows, or a racecourse at a nineteenth-century fair — would crown the new European galleries. Just the type of art you'd expect people like Victor, shopping-mall magnate and racehorse owner, to buy. Uninterested in art before 1900, she assumed that the theme of the chairman's collection originated from his predatory attitude toward retail complexes and that he identified with the mounted hunters looking down on a cornered fox.

Amanda entered George's office to find him staring morosely at a newspaper spread open on his desk. She recognized the *Tribune*.

"Hello, George. Happy with Kinsella's article? It gives the campaign launch a profile."

"Hmph." George threw the paper aside, shifting a blue folder as he did so, then gestured to his guest chair. Amanda sat, deciding not to press the director on his grumpy reply. She suspected that Kinsella's dredging up *Monet's Moments* and the gallery's name change needled George at a time when he wanted TAG to shine.

"I'm looking forward to talking about the new galleries tomorrow. Did you need some information for your speech?" She wondered what this meeting was about.

"No, thanks. It's short. We're all speaking briefly," George said, avoiding her eyes. "But I'll be making an announcement and I wanted to tell you about it first."

"Oh?" Amanda tried to sound pleasantly interested, but she couldn't shake a feeling of foreboding.

"The sculpture commission." George took a deep breath. "It's going to Daniel Reid."

Amanda's eyes widened and her head jerked backward. She stared at the director with her mouth partly open. How dare he decide on the artist for the commission without her input. And to give it to an American, at that. Yet another privileged white male. She pictured a huge rusted-steel shape dominating the new space, as opposed to the airy floating construction that Simone Brodeur could produce. She sat up and squared her jaw.

"Daniel Reid? How was this decided? And when? How could you do this?" she asked, her voice rising on the last question. She couldn't think of a single meeting that had even mentioned the sculpture commission. In her mind, it sat on the back burner until the fundraising ignited but under her control. How dare George think he could just take over!

"You remember we met him at the Armory Show," said George, referring to New York's annual art fair held in March. He folded his arms and leaned back in his chair. "With Victor and Zach," he added. Zachary Drake was Victor's son. He ran an affordable fashion chain called ZAD, conveniently located in prime spots in his father's retail malls. Amanda thought he was an uncultured swine with delusions of artistic taste. That night at the Armory Show, Amanda *had* noticed the camaraderie that quickly developed between the four men, but there must have been even more to it than she'd thought. When she'd left them to meet a curator at the Museum of Modern Art, she must have provided them with the perfect opportunity to cook up this scheme over cocktails. "Zach admires his work a lot. Reid's a high-profile artist. It's a coup for us to get his first sculpture commission in Toronto."

"I know he's high-profile, but what does Zach have to do with it? George, this is a contemporary issue. I'm the curator of contemporary art. I'm the one who should be proposing artists for this commission, not having a done deal forced on me."

When Victor was named chairman of the board, Zach had started to appear at gallery events. Amanda wasn't sure if his father wanted him to acquire some gravitas to offset his playboy image or if Zach saw contemporary art as an extension of his fashion and design world. George's ego, easily stroked by being around important artists and wealthy supporters, was often motivated to make generous promises — promises she sometimes had to recalibrate. But he had never transgressed so far onto her territory before. It was outrageous.

"I know you're the curator of contemporary art, Amanda," said George, glancing away from her reddening face. "And you'll be making terrific acquisitions for the new galleries. But the foyer of the new wing is a statement space. We need an outstanding work there."

"You think I can't find an artist who can make a statement?" Amanda asked incredulously. Then she paused. "Wait a minute. Is

Zach funding this commission? You've made a deal with him, haven't you? His artist for his money. I bet you've even promised to name the damned space after him!"

"That's preposterous," said George, leaping up to stand beside his desk and loom over Amanda. "We have a scale of naming rights based on the amount donated to the campaign. We won't be naming any galleries until we see what people give."

"Well, is he funding the commission?" When the director remained silent, Amanda burst out, "George, that's not the procedure."

"Look, I called you in here as a courtesy, to inform you—"

"A courtesy!" Amanda jumped up and stood at the other side of George's desk. "Some courtesy! You're overstepping your boundaries. Does Roger know about this? I thought we had a curatorial process." Amanda didn't really care if the chief curator knew about this travesty or not, as she preferred to bypass him and make a beeline for the director as much as she could. So yeah, maybe she flouted the official process now and again, but for George to do so in such a blatantly aggravating way? She wouldn't stand for it.

"I'll make sure Roger knows," George said, placing his hands on his hips. "I need to have a chat with him about your budgets too. That last show overspent, as usual."

Amanda's mouth gaped open for a moment, then clamped shut. She demanded the best for her exhibitions and was far too busy to oversee their budgets. She'd always assumed George understood that and found funds elsewhere to balance the books. But she refused to get distracted by his accusation. "I thought we'd agreed to get the campaign going before tackling this commission."

"What have you got against Daniel Reid, anyway?"

"That's not the point. You should not be approaching artists without my involvement."

"You haven't spoken to anyone else yet?" George asked, eyeing her pointedly.

Amanda looked away. God, Simone. What would she tell her? "No, I know it's too soon. I've been thinking about it, though. I wanted to be ready when the time came."

"Well, then, it's no problem. I'll announce it tomorrow. Should generate a lot of buzz. Might even inspire some of your collectors to donate." George walked back to his desk and sat down, signalling that the meeting was over. "I'd appreciate your support on this. It's good for the gallery and for your department."

Amanda seethed. She didn't care about Victor and his horse paintings, but Zach and a hot-shot American sculptor was too much. Placing her fists on the edge of the desk, she leaned in, ready to do some looming of her own.

"This is completely unacceptable, and you know it. I'm insulted that you think you can make major decisions about my area without consulting me. The board will hear about it." But even as she said it, she knew her threat sounded hollow.

"And I think the board will agree that the new wing needs a major sculpture. I've paid you the courtesy of telling you about it before it's announced publicly. In case you've forgotten, Amanda, I'm the director of TAG. I'm not asking for your permission. I expect your support on this." He stuck out his chin with determination, but his eyes flicked away.

Amanda glared at him for a moment, then looked down at the desk to gather her thoughts. As she struggled with her reply, her gaze fixed on some papers sticking out of the blue folder. One of them had letterhead saying "Hathaway." In spite of her agitation, she wondered why that name rang a bell. George slid the folder toward himself, obscuring her view.

"That's all," he said. "You can go."

She took a deep breath. "I want the new wing as much as you do, George. I still think this decision is outrageous, but I'll keep it to myself because I want the gala to go well. But I won't forget this."

She turned and left the office, ignoring George's irritable, "Neither will I."

Amanda marched to the stairs and ran down. Relieved to reach her office without seeing anyone, she shut the door, then collapsed at her desk. So much for her close relationship with the director. She'd assumed they were on the same wavelength. What would she tell Simone? For a few minutes, she stared at the wall, wrestling with her anger.

Then her gaze focused on the folders on her desk, and she drew the plan of the new wing toward her. She remembered something Simone had told her, something about an artists' collective she had been invited to speak to. Invited by Justin, one of the installation technicians at TAG. Amanda reached for her rolodex. Time to have a chat with Justin, who had so competently handled the many technical demands placed on him by *Gestes*.

CHAPTER 3
ARTHUR

The silver maple trees in the small park behind TAG were starting to bud, but Arthur Matlock did not notice that sign of spring as he walked back from lunch. As curator of Canadian historical art, he was accustomed to unexpected issues popping up to disturb his routine of research and writing — a spike in a gallery's humidity level or a call from a member of the public eager to convince him that their precious painting would add lustre to TAG's collection. But the task he'd taken on for tomorrow night won the prize for most unusual and least wanted of them all.

At forty-two, Arthur resembled a genial university professor with his stooped shoulders, unfashionably long graying hair creeping over his collar, and wire-rimmed glasses. His current project was an exhibition of works owned by old friends of his, Alastair and Margaret Ramsay, who had amassed oils, watercolours, and drawings by some of the leading Canadian artists of the period from 1870 to 1914. The exhibition had been in the works for ages, but the planning process hadn't been without compromise. In fact, he had shocked himself with the lengths to which he would go to secure the show.

He fell into step with his boss, Roger Laplante, as they entered the gallery together.

"Hi, Arthur. Looking forward to tomorrow?" asked the chief curator.

"Somewhat. I'll be glad when the tour's over."

"Tour?" Roger frowned. "Ahh, yes. That tour. Ms. Ramsay's request. I'd forgotten that it will happen tomorrow night. Rather a full schedule. By the way, does George know about it?"

Arthur looked at Roger with surprise. "He knows that it's her condition for lending her paintings for the exhibition, and he knows how important it is to have the whole collection. I told him when it was confirmed two months ago."

They entered the elevator and Roger pressed the third-floor button.

"Hmm. The things we have to do for patrons. I think our revered chairman is finally content that his horses and fox hunts will have the splendour they deserve in the new wing. We curators have to work with what comes our way. *C'est la vie.*" Roger shrugged.

As they left the elevator, Arthur thought that Roger's challenges were easier than his. Accommodating Victor Drake's demands at least still sat within a chief curator's mandate, but what he had to do for Barbara Ramsay leapt into unknown territory. He thought back to the family dinner in Kingston two years ago, when Margaret and Alastair had invited him to discuss the loan of the complete collection.

***

"Why should I lend my paintings?" said Barbara sullenly. "You've all been plotting without me. You can't just assume I'll agree."

"Oh, for Christ's sake," snapped Alex, her brother. Arthur's best friend since high school, he had already committed his four works. "We've all got better things to do than plot against you. You know Mom and Dad contacted you when Art first approached them. You were probably too blitzed out in Hawaii, or wherever you were, to remember. Can't you just grow up and agree to lend your paintings so Art can get on with his work?"

"Stop bullying me, Alex," said Barbara, twirling a perfectly streaked strand of red-gold hair in her long fingers.

Arthur's apprehension about this hitch in his exhibition's progress was overtaken for a moment by overwhelming attraction. At first he had known Barbara just as his pal Alex's kid sister, a teasing, spoiled adolescent who wormed her way into their boat rides and campfires on idyllic summer vacations at the Ramsays' cottage. In university, Arthur visited less often, so Barbara's development into a beautiful young woman astonished him on the few times their paths crossed. While he still considered Alex a close friend, Arthur felt that Barbara had propelled out of his orbit, as her playfulness morphed into restlessness that burned through two marriages. On the rare occasions when he had seen her on the arm of one husband or the other, she had always been friendly but a bit distracted, as if she didn't know how to place Arthur in her current circle. According to Alex's dismissive accounts, her generous divorce settlements enabled her to freely chase errant whims, often at the cost of seeing her daughter from her second marriage.

Arthur was quite sure Barbara didn't care what her family thought of her way of life. In fact, she likely considered them plodding and boringly stable, and he suspected that she included him in that assessment, too, if she even gave him any thought. His own long-term relationships with women had amicably petered out due to the challenges of careers and distance. While his curatorial ambition drove his wish to show the Ramsays' collection, he was surprised by how much he looked forward to reconnecting with Barbara through the process.

"They're not even your favourite style. You won't miss them for a few months," said Alex in the same irritated tone. They all knew that she preferred the abstract paintings she'd acquired with part of her first divorce settlement to the realistic images bestowed by her parents. Arthur couldn't see why she'd be loath to part with them for a time. Her manner — fiddling with her hair, casting her well-made-up green eyes coolly from one to another — suggested she wasn't seriously going to refuse, but rather that she enjoyed toying with their expectations. He sat up as she turned her dazzling gaze toward him.

"I want to hear from Art why my paintings are so crucial," she said, leaning toward him with a half-smile. Feeling a bit like a dishevelled schoolboy hauled before a haughty yet elegant school principal, Arthur launched into his well-honed pitch regarding the art historical value of the Ramsay collection, the scholarly contributions it would make, the importance of showing it in its entirety, and the pride the gallery would take in hosting its first public unveiling. He edited his spiel a bit for Barbara's benefit, suspecting that she would lose interest if he delved into too many scholarly details. Instead, he adopted the style used in the gallery's media releases, which had a knack for summarizing content into bite-size chunks. From Barbara's intent, surprised look, he assumed he'd hit the right tone. She threw up her arms.

"Okay, you've convinced me. You obviously know your stuff, Art. I'll lend them." Everyone smiled as Alex reached for the bottle of Prosecco on the coffee table.

"Great! Let's drink to that," he said.

"On one condition," continued Barbara. Alex stopped untwisting the wire cover, Margaret froze with the tray of glasses, and Alastair looked up at the ceiling as if to ask the ornate plaster medallion why his daughter was not more like his dependable son.

"What's that, Barbara?" asked Arthur calmly. "Thank you, by the way. On behalf of the gallery, I have to say we're very grateful for your generosity and assure you that your paintings will receive excellent care and handling. And we always try to accommodate lenders' requests." In Arthur's field, such asks tended to be modest and easily fulfilled — a few dinners, free catalogues, exclusive tours, or complimentary tickets for friends and family to attend the exhibition and programs.

"I wouldn't expect anything less, Art. You obviously work for a highly professional organization," she replied with a smile.

"Well, what is it?" asked Alex. "We're getting thirsty here."

"I was in Hawaii recently. Not blitzed out and forgetful, as you implied, dear brother, but appreciating a new experience." Barbara tossed her shoulder-length hair and looked dreamily at the paintings covering the far wall of her parents' living room. "I was on a yoga retreat in the mountains."

"So, you want to do yoga in the gallery, dear?" asked Margaret, more sensitive to her daughter's moods than her husband and son.

"It was a nude yoga retreat," continued Barbara.

"Oh Christ," muttered Alex, resuming his removal of the wire cage around the Prosecco cork.

"I'm sure it was an interesting experience, but what does it have to do with the gallery?" asked Arthur, a feeling of dread rising in his chest.

"Well, the leader runs a naturist group in Toronto, which I've joined. They're always looking for things to do and not all places are open to their particular needs. I want to help them. I think they'd like a tour of the gallery."

"Oh, well, we do tours all the time," said Arthur, relieved. "But—"

"Wait a minute, Sis," interrupted Alex. "Are you saying this group of nudists—"

"Naturists," snapped Barbara.

"Naturists," sighed Alex. "Are you saying they're going to come au naturel? Does Art have to participate likewise?"

"Yes, we'll take off our clothes when we get there and enjoy the tour in the buff," said Barbara. "Gallery staff can keep their clothes on. We're used to that. Is that possible, Art? It's just my one little request." Arthur's absorption in her flirtatious gaze almost made him miss the eye-rolling exchange between Alex and his father.

"Little!" scoffed Alex. "Don't you think that's imposing on the gallery just a bit? They're going to have to make special arrangements. Is it even possible, Art?"

"Well, it's unusual, but I don't see that it's impossible. I'll relay the request to my colleagues," said Arthur quickly. For a terrifying moment he'd imagined himself leading a tour in the nude, lending the word "exhibition" a meaning far beyond its usual interpretation. Reassured, he wanted to settle the issue. "They might want to meet you and work out the details when you come in to sign the loan agreement. I know everyone will be thrilled when I tell them we have the collection in its entirety."

Alex expertly twisted out the cork from the well-chilled bottle.

"You'll get the first glass, Art," he said. "I think you deserve it after all that."

***

If Arthur had deserved a drink then, he certainly merited the whole bottle by now. The tour had first been scheduled fourteen months ago, just before what was to be the Ramsay show's original opening, but then George had bumped the show to accommodate that silly *Monet's Moments* thing.

Originally called *Paintings from the Musée Martin,* the exhibition's mundane title had provoked a critical reaction from the head of marketing and communications. "Those haystacks look like muffins. Let's call it *Monet's Muffins: Impressionist Paintings,*" she said. Arthur had to admit that the show's signature work, a haystack drenched with a sunset's golden rays, bore some resemblance to a pointy walnut muffin that had oozed over its paper cup while baking, but he dreaded the thought of scholars mocking the conflation of a common North American snack food with one of Monet's famous studies of light. Fortunately, even the director could not swallow the alleged popular appeal of that title, and the show became *Monet's Moments.*

"The Impressionist show will make a good profit, which can go toward the expansion plans," George told him at the time. "I'm sure you can assure the Ramsays that we still want to present their collection, just at a better time for the gallery."

Of course, Barbara took offence and cancelled the date. Arthur's attempt to mollify her by taking her to dinner had failed, as she only talked about her yoga teacher. Since then, Arthur's secretary had persisted in trying to reschedule, hampered by Barbara's frequent absences. She continued to make the naturist tour her condition for loaning the paintings, and she insisted that tomorrow night was the only time that the group could make it.

After exhibiting some surprise and disappointment, the elder Ramsays resigned themselves to the postponement, to Arthur's relief. Margaret and Alastair still thought enough of the gallery to purchase tickets for the gala tomorrow night.

Tomorrow night! Arthur snapped out of his musings. As he entered his office, he pondered yet again how his years of research, curating, and public speaking had brought him to the faintly ludicrous prospect of leading a tour for naturists. He bet that the Canadian curator at the National Gallery didn't have to put up with this. Few lenders required as careful a touch as Barbara did. Oops, better rephrase that. No touching allowed in this situation.

Of course, Barbara wanted to see more than the Canadian rooms so, as the other curators would all be attending the reception and dinner, Arthur had contacted education for help in touring some of the contemporary area. He expected the acting head to leap at the opportunity, although he couldn't remember now if he had actually confirmed his participation.

A knock at the door distracted him from this train of thought. It was his secretary, holding a plastic-wrapped book. "The Ramsay catalogue. It's arrived early," she said, handing him a copy of *Terrain and Town: The Ramsay Canadian Collection.*

Arthur's anxiety disappeared as he thanked her and ripped off the shrink wrap. He raised the catalogue to his face and inhaled the crisp smell of printer's ink and fresh paper. He set it on his desk and stroked its glossy cover, on which gleamed the greens and rusts of an enlarged detail of Talbot's *Bend, Rideau River*. A rush of pride at this first product of years of toil made him smile. He knew he had written an excellent catalogue to accompany an outstanding exhibition and couldn't wait to give Margaret and Alastair their advance copy tomorrow evening. He allowed himself to hope that even Barbara would be impressed.

CHAPTER 4
RACHEL

Rachel Burns approached the front doors of the Harbord Bistro just as the hostess unlocked them. Grateful to get out of the April rain, she closed her umbrella and walked to her favourite spot by the window. She loved this restaurant, with its marble-topped bar, French posters on the brick-red walls, and vintage wooden tables. For a moment she thought of ordering a Perrier while she waited for her friend to join her, but that didn't last. She deserved a drink now.

"I'll have a glass of the house red," she said to the waiter. She gazed out the window. Passersby jostled with their umbrellas along Harbord Street, but Rachel barely noticed them. She was preoccupied with the events of the afternoon. The interview had gone so well.

At thirty-nine, Rachel coloured her dark-brown, shoulder-length hair and occasionally hit the gym to fight a slight midriff bulge. She didn't see any crow's feet around her blue eyes yet. She had chosen one of her classic black pantsuits today, an outfit she often wore in her work at TAG, where she was the coordinator of adult programs. Rachel used to love her job, which she'd held for her nine years at the gallery. She organized lectures and programs to accompany exhibitions, gave talks, and supervised the docents who delivered most of the public tours. For years, Thomas, the head of the department, had been something of a mentor. He had supported Rachel's professional development, and everyone thought he'd put in a good word for her as his successor. But then, five months ago, he retired, and Rachel's hopes for a new challenge sank when her colleague Jeremy Singer became acting head of education and public programs.

Rachel chafed so much under Jeremy's prickly and self-interested leadership that his surname morphed in her mind to "Stinger." Torn between a desire to apply for the permanent head job herself and a need to escape Jeremy, she had grown impatient with the delay in posting the position and started looking elsewhere. Today she had called in sick to attend a job interview at the university art gallery.

She looked forward to telling Carolyn, an old friend from grad school, all about it. While Rachel had always worked in the Toronto area, Carolyn had moved around the country, ending up as head of education in a Calgary gallery. Now on a visit to Ontario, she had set up some meetings with educators, including Jeremy.

The waiter brought Rachel's wine and she quickly took a sip, then rose to hug Carolyn.

"Rachel, it's great to see you! You've already started. I'd better catch up. Shall we get a bottle?"

The order given, Carolyn folded her arms on the table and leaned toward Rachel.

"I want to hear all about it. I don't know why you'd want to leave TAG, but tell me about the interview."

"I'm still processing it, but I think it went really well. I wasn't stymied by any of their questions. They made me talk about a work in their collection, which I aced. It just seemed to flow. And I liked them." Rachel drank some wine.

"I'm not surprised. If I know you, you prepared like hell."

"Probably over-prepared," said Rachel with a chuckle. "Nick got fed up with rehearsing me through the questions. He said I was putting more effort into this interview than he had to do for a trial." Rachel's husband, Nick, was a criminal lawyer.

"How is Nick? I bet he'd rather rehearse his band than your interview. What's their name again?" Nick belonged to a hobby rock band with four other middle-aged lawyers.

"The Briefs," replied Rachel.

"The Briefs! Hah! Great name for a bunch of lawyers. Did you come up with it?"

"I did. They said, 'It's almost edgy enough for us.' They haven't had to use it much, actually, but they've got a fortieth-birthday celebration coming up. I won't see much of him for the next week or so. Rehearsing."

"I wish I could hear them, but I'll be back in Calgary by then."

As the waiter brought the bottle of Merlot and served it, Rachel listened to Carolyn's account of a staff conflict waiting for her attention when she returned to work. *Sounds like TAG*, she thought. Part of her motivation for applying to other jobs was Nick's frustration with her complaints. He was sympathetic and supportive, but she knew she had tried his patience with her rants about Jeremy. That damn Stinger. He might drive her away from TAG, but she couldn't let him ruin her marriage. *Get a grip. Nick wouldn't let her get away with such hyperbole.*

Carolyn interrupted her story to take a gulp of wine. "That hit the spot."

"Now it's your turn. Tell me about your meeting with Jeremy," said Rachel, feeling a flutter in her stomach. Hunger or nervousness? She wondered what Jeremy might say behind her back, unaware that she and Carolyn were friends.

"Like I said, I couldn't believe that you'd want to leave TAG until I met him. He was nice enough, after he kept me waiting ten minutes, but he barely answered my question about labels and went on and on about some visitor engagement centre he wants to build. It sounds like he thinks he's the fucking director."

Rachel laughed, as she usually did at hearing Carolyn's no-nonsense take on people. She wasn't surprised that Jeremy had seized the chance to expound on his latest vision. He'd been steadily raising his profile since he'd joined TAG two years ago in the new interpretive planning section. The planning team worked closely with the curators on the exhibitions, producing material to help visitors engage with the art, such as label content, brochures, audioguides, and informative videos. Sometimes they stepped into creating programs, which overlapped with Rachel's job, resulting in clashes with Jeremy. His hopes for a visitor engagement centre — potentially a big room with computers, videos, art-making stations, hands-on activities, and listening pods — indicated his ambition had risen to a new level.

"So you haven't succumbed to his charisma?" she asked as the waiter poured her some Merlot and removed her empty first glass. That was fast.

"No," snorted Carolyn. "I asked him if the visitor engagement centre was confirmed, but he just blustered on about how he's an advocate for the visitor and the new wing needs it."

"That's one of his favourite phrases," said Rachel. "As if he's the only one in education who could possibly understand what visitors need. I'm not surprised he blustered. The centre's not a sure thing in the new wing, even though I know he's looking for funding. Where does he get the gall?"

Carolyn shrugged, then looked at Rachel seriously. "I was surprised that they didn't make you acting head. You've been there a lot longer."

"The senior managers seem to like him, so he got the promotion."

"And that was last October? That's a long time to have an acting head position," said Carolyn over the rim of her wineglass.

"Not at TAG. Not these days. The director and everyone are so focused on our big gala tomorrow night, they can't be bothered to post the permanent job. I want to apply, but I'm getting tired of waiting. And the university job looks good, so I figured I'd better plan an escape route. Should we look at the menu?" Her lunch seemed a long time ago.

"Oh, I'm going to have what I always have here. Steak frites. They're the best," Carolyn said, pushing aside her menu. When their waiter returned to tell them the specials, Carolyn almost interrupted him to order her salad and steak and Rachel took the easy route by seconding it. She felt too discombobulated to give the menu any attention — still on a high from her interview, but feeling the usual tension when she talked about Jeremy.

"He's a piece of work," said Carolyn. "But still, you said you have to escape. That's pretty serious. What's he done to you?"

"He disses my ideas, then takes credit for them when senior management likes them." Rachel paused. She had never phrased it so succinctly. She saw Carolyn's eyes widen and launched into her case against Jeremy.

First, there was *Perspectives*. The gallery faced demands to broaden its Eurocentric collection and exhibitions, so Rachel developed a program called *Perspectives*, in which she invited members of the city's diverse communities to provide insight on works in TAG's permanent collection. Months of outreach to groups — Afro-Caribbean, Asian, Indigenous, gay, and others — had gradually overcome their resistance and lack of familiarity with the gallery. Eventually, people willing to offer a new commentary emerged, they chose key works to discuss, and Rachel enjoyed shaping a dialogue-based tour with them. The attendance proved as varied as she had hoped — members of the invited communities, but also people from the broader public who welcomed a fresh take on some familiar works. Rachel was so gratified by the program's success that she submitted it for a national Museum Education award.

While she waited to hear about the possible recognition of her talents, she was sucked into the vortex that was Jeremy's biggest profile-raising venture to date. He convinced the previous head, Thomas, to let the department run an international conference, *The Museum Summit*, to bring scholars and museum professionals together to discuss the role of the art museum today.

"When I asked him, 'Isn't the title a little grandiose?', you won't believe what he said."

"Let me think," said Carolyn, putting an index finger to her chin and assuming a thoughtful expression. "Something motivational like 'Don't be afraid of reaching new heights.'"

"I wish it was that positive. He said, 'Nobody here knows anything about education and visitor engagement. It's a good thing I'm bringing in these experts, so it will change.' Jerk! Not only did he diss us, but also Tom's twenty years at the gallery. Then he added insult to injury by saying that he'd lined up some people I should speak to because 'They can really help you understand the opportunities surrounding adult programs.'" Rachel spat out this last sentence and took a swig of wine.

"Meanwhile, *Perspectives* was up for a prestigious award, right?" Carolyn watched as the waiter placed some bread in the basket hanging above them, then she deftly pulled at the ropes to lower it to their level. They each took a slice. "I love these baskets. That's why we had to eat here."

Rachel nodded, oblivious to Carolyn's enjoyment of the bistro's charm. Wound up and grateful for the chance to vent about Stinger to an old friend who also knew the field, she continued with the summit saga. Jeremy had garnered an impressive amount of funding, which allowed them to invite high-profile international speakers. Unfortunately, the lion's share of money went to the guests' honoraria, accommodations, and travel, with no allocation for hiring a conference coordinator. The education staff shouldered the tasks, on top of their regular jobs, which Rachel gamely accepted until she realized that as she drowned in organizational minutiae, Jeremy hovered in the more intellectually rewarding realm of producing the summit content. His networking ensured that prominent galleries sent their interpretive planners.

"And, of course, he loved telling me that the Museum of Modern Art thought we're doing the most innovative visitor engagement in North America. They wanted him to make a presentation to their staff."

Carolyn rolled her eyes, then smiled at the waiter as their salads arrived.

"I know you're hanging on every word," said Rachel, "but I need some food. I just had a sandwich because I was nervous before the interview." She chewed one mouthful before her need to vent took over. She told Carolyn that she had organized a well-received panel discussion with local educators, in between conferring with the gallery chef about dietary requirements for the lunches or reminding the financial department about honorarium cheques. She'd done all she could to support the summit, but had hoped that Tom was keeping tabs on the expenses. Jeremy's self-image did not include such mundane worries.

Two weeks later, Jeremy spent his first week as acting head in New York, fulfilling his summit networking. As he buzzed around several museum education departments, Rachel toiled away at compiling her department's contribution to the gallery's annual application to the provincial arts council for funding. After cajoling her colleagues for statistics and information, she laboured long hours to meet the administration's deadline.

"So he gets back from his triumphant trip and all he can say when he looked at what I'd written was 'I wouldn't do it this way, but I suppose it's all right. You're on top of the details, Rachel, but it needs some big picture thinking. I'll add that so George knows how visionary we are.'"

"Rachel, you're propping him up while he gets the glory," Carolyn said with a note of reproach, laying her fork on her empty salad plate. Rachel was only halfway through hers.

Rachel nodded. "I know. And I'm sick of it. The final straw was when George — our director — announced the winner of the Museum Education award. He sent an all-staff email. He congratulated the department but singled out Jeremy: 'Jeremy's program *Perspectives* represents the direction that TAG should be taking and deserves high praise.'" She adopted another snarky tone for this last sentence, then stabbed a tomato slice. "It was my program. But he got to go to Ottawa and collect the award."

"You know, I noticed the plaque on his wall, so I asked him which of his staff had developed the program. Of course, I knew that you had. Know what he said?"

Rachel looked at Carolyn glumly. Here was the moment she had feared. Carolyn put down her glass and continued.

"He said that it proved the summit was necessary, because all those progressive speakers he brought here had helped his adult programs coordinator to carry out his idea! When I said that a program like *Perspectives* must have taken months of organization, he fobbed me off on one of his staff to talk about labels! What a self-important prick. He's not nicknamed Stinger for nothing."

"As in the queen bee sticking it to the worker," moaned Rachel, provoking a sympathy pout from Carolyn.

"Stinker would fit just as well. Do you think he'll become the head of the department?"

"God help me," said Rachel, refilling their glasses. "I think he thinks so."

"I've just remembered. When he was going on about that visitor engagement centre, he said things like 'when I'm head' or 'my plans for the department,' then caught himself. He sure sounded like he didn't think there was any internal competition. He said something about getting rid of docents too. That would affect your job, right?"

"You bet. He just wants everyone hooked up to audioguides or watching his videos," said Rachel. "There's a place for that, of course, but TAG has to draw a wide audience. There are still people who like lectures and guided tours." She put her fork down. The waiter swooped in to remove their plates. "The irony is, I'd like to work on an audioguide or a video sometime, but it's so specialized at TAG that I can't. I'd have more scope if I went to the university art gallery."

"More scope and more work, if you're the one-person department," said Carolyn with a wry smile. "Oh good. I'm looking forward to this." Their steak frites arrived.

"I don't want to work with someone who's only out for himself and not a team player. I hate the thought of leaving TAG. I love the collection and most of the people I work with. But Jeremy's just an energy-draining, narcissistic monster."

Carolyn dipped a fry into the garlic mayonnaise, then pointed it at Rachel. "Monster? That's over the top. I think you mean asshole. Watch out. You're letting him get under your skin." She ate the fry. "Yum! This is so good."

"That's what Nick says. He's got a new defensive strategy when he catches me starting a rant. He holds up his hand and declares 'J-word-free zone.' It works. I laugh."

"Thank goodness for Nick," said Carolyn with a smile. More seriously, she added, "You've got a lot to give, Rachel. I think it's too bad, but I can see why you're looking elsewhere."

Rachel tucked into her steak. She listened as Carolyn recounted some gossip about other museum educators they knew, grateful for a reprieve from talking about her situation. Her friend was right. It was unfortunate that she felt she had to leave TAG after nine good years, but she couldn't remain at a job that was all stress and no satisfaction.

Carolyn insisted on having a nightcap at a bar on Bloor Street, so it was almost eleven when they staggered onto the sidewalk to look for taxis.

"It was great to see you again, Rachel," said Carolyn, hugging her. "But promise me one thing. However long you stay at TAG, you won't keep doing Stinger's dirty work for him."

Blearily, Rachel picked up on her friend's concern and agreed.

FRIDAY

CHAPTER 5
GEORGE

On Friday morning, George picked up the night's agenda and familiarized himself with the order of events:

6:00 – Valet parking staff arrive.

6:30 – Guests arrive. Champagne and canapé reception in the sculpture hall. Architectural model and drawings unveiled. Jazz trio plays.

7:20 – Guests move to Littlewood Court for sit-down dinner.

7:30 – Short speeches from George, Victor, and the architect of the new wing.

7:45 – Wait staff serve appetizers. Pianist plays.

8:00 – Entrées served.

8:30 – Contemporary dance troupe performs.

9:00 – Dessert in Littlewood Court. Coffee and liqueurs in sculpture gallery. Staff from the development department at discreetly placed tables for those so moved to make their financial pledges on the spot.

10:30 – The end.

A perfectly planned evening, he thought. He looked up as John Theodorakis, TAG's deputy director, entered his office for his weekly briefing. Like a queen bee fed royal jelly by the workers, George expected all reports from senior managers to nurture his sense of command, especially today. His phone rang.

"Yes, Victor, I know they're coming. No, there's no need for you to come early to check the setup. It'll be fine. See you at six-fifteen."

John raised his eyebrows as he sat down across from his boss. "Victor showing his usual confidence in our organization?"

George frowned. Although he was getting tired of Victor's micromanaging, he resented John's sarcasm regarding the board chair. "He just wanted to make sure I know the Haddads are coming. He's sure they're good for five million. Doesn't matter that we went over everything yesterday. But it's a big night for Victor. First special event under his chairmanship. And he's chair of the campaign."

"Not to mention he's announcing his pledge to the campaign and his art donation," said John, fingering a sheet of paper in his hand. "Victor's become very generous in a short period of time."

"Well, we need philanthropic board members," said George. Surely John realized that he and Victor worked well together. He leaned forward. "I've got a good feeling about tonight. We sold the last ticket two weeks ago. Full house. Every big name we wanted will be here. Exclusive event, advance look at the new wing. We'll get some good pledges."

John nodded politely, but George could tell that his interest in the gala and its implications did not equal his own. With a distracted air, George had listened to his deputy's briefings about the gallery's mundane problems and issues — the latest union grievances, the stalled job postings, temperature fluctuations in the Canadian wing, the need for improved coordination of the many events and programs — his mind on the model crowning the table across the room. But George considered John a good lieutenant, supporting his general in all his campaigns, from the changing of the gallery's name to making a last-minute grab for *Monet's Moments*. He had overheard John continue to call it *Monet's Muffins*, and suspected that his deputy considered the project a half-baked scheme causing an indigestible number of problems, from increased security to expensive changes to advertising and promotion. But he valued John's ability to keep TAG humming along like a beehive, even if the public did not always eagerly devour the cultural nourishment it offered.

John shifted in his chair. George stroked the ring on his right hand, a talisman of command and control, and wondered why his deputy looked uncomfortable. *John needs his own ring*, he thought. *This is just a routine meeting. Let's get on with it.*

As if sensing his boss's impatience, John frowned at the piece of paper in his hand, the daily schedule of events, just received from the Head of Security, and said, "Um, there's a few things to go over."

"Shoot."

"There are two other events going on tonight. Arthur's got that, umm, nudist, I mean naturist tour from seven to eight thirty—"

"What?!"

"Barbara Ramsay's naturist tour is happening from seven to eight thirty—"

"Are you fucking kidding me?"

John flinched at George's shout, but kept his eyes focused on the paper in his hand.

"Apparently education has some new program too," he continued. "A sleepover thing with kids. They'll arrive at five thirty and stay all night."

"Fucking fuck!" George recoiled from his desk, his chair bumping against the mahogany credenza behind him. "How the hell did that happen? This event is supposed to be exclusive!" He sprang up from his chair and strode around to loom over John, who remained seated. George believed that looming was an effective management tactic, if not one endorsed by Harvard. "Who let in these other damn things?"

John glanced up, then back at the sheet of paper.

"The naturist tour is a donor request, you'll remember. Barbara Ramsay. Arthur agreed to do it so she would lend her paintings for the show next month. For obvious reasons, it had to be scheduled when the gallery isn't open to the public."

"Never mind the public! What about the hundred potential campaign donors who think they're coming to an exclusive event?" barked George. He dimly remembered Arthur telling him about this tour. Trust him to have such a wacko donor. "We can't have a bunch of naked people roaming around. We'll be a laughingstock."

"I've spoken to security about it—"

"How the hell did you let this happen? Haven't I stressed how important tonight is? Why am I just hearing about these damn things now?"

"Look, George, I've been saying we need to coordinate events better," said John in a resentful tone. "I gather Arthur's been trying to confirm this tour for two years, but Ms. Ramsay cancelled when the show was postponed last year by *Monet's Muf... Moments*, and this was the only date she'd agree to." He looked at his boss with a smug expression, as if relishing the fact that bumping the Ramsay show caused a few more ripples to wash up on the director's exalted shore.

"Arthur's taken two years on this tour? No wonder I call him Arthur Deadlock! He's not my most dynamic curator, but this is ridiculous. Fucking incompetent!"

"You know donor relations can be tricky. We're expecting the arrival of the Ramsay works on Tuesday, so Arthur probably wanted to get this out of the way. Good thing I get these daily reports."

"Great bloody timing," spat George, as he paced around the office. He stopped beside the architectural model and turned back to John. "What was the other thing — kids?"

"Evidently museums are getting into sleepovers and Jeremy wants to pilot one."

"Sleepovers! You're not serious!" George banged his fist on the table, causing a splintering sound. John swivelled to see slivers of balsa wood and foamcore where the new wing had formerly stood.

"Shit!" George cast an irritated look at his deputy, who had averted his eyes. He glanced back at the model, then strode to his chair. "Why does the damn pilot have to be tonight?"

"Not sure, but I just found out that marketing's been working with education because they want TV coverage…"

"TV coverage! That's all we need — TV cameras exposing this scheduling shit show. Christ! It's bad enough that Arthur's walking around with his head in the clouds, and now I have bloody education trying to ruin my event? Get Arthur and Jeremy in here. Now."

Stung by George's angry tone, John hurried to comply.

CHAPTER 6
ARTHUR

Arthur walked down the hall, nearly colliding with Jeremy Singer as he strode off the elevator. The two men looked at each other in surprise when they realized they were walking in the same direction.

"Hi, Arthur. Looking forward to tonight?" asked Jeremy.

"I assume you mean the gala. I'm certainly looking forward to seeing the Ramsays, once my part of that ridiculous tour is over," said Arthur with a shudder. "Thanks again for taking over the rest."

Jeremy was about to reply when he caught sight of the deputy director standing at George's door, looking impatient.

"Come on, then," said John in a tone that implied he'd been waiting hours instead of ten minutes. He ushered them in, pointed at two chairs, shut the door, and remained standing by it, like a taciturn sentinel. *Or a prison guard*, Arthur thought warily.

George was on the phone, but he acknowledged the newcomers with a ferocious glare. "I assure you, Victor, we're on top of it. Sorry, but I've got a situation here… No, nothing to do with tonight. Don't worry. Everything's under control. See you later." He slammed the receiver down. Arthur and Jeremy's polite smiles faded.

"What the hell are you two playing at?" he thundered immediately. Arthur flinched and shot a worried look at Jeremy.

"You know me, George," said Arthur slowly. "I don't generally play at all. Could you please tell us what this is about?"

"It's about tonight," said George, rising to walk around to the front of his desk. With arms folded, he stared down at his two employees menacingly. Jeremy shifted in his chair. Arthur did his best to remain impassive while his stomach fluttered uncomfortably.

"Do you two numbskulls have any idea how important this gala event is? This expansion, a project that will ensure the continued viability of this gallery, a project with which I assume all staff are aligned, will require us to raise a hundred and fifty million dollars. The federal and provincial governments have promised thirty million. Our exceedingly generous board chairman, who believes strongly in this endeavour, will announce his gift of ten million dollars tonight. That means we still need to raise a hundred and ten million dollars. ONE HUNDRED AND TEN MILLION DOLLARS. How do you suppose we are going to raise that money, hm? Would you like to make a donation, Arthur? Are you a secret millionaire, Jeremy? This exclusive gala reception and dinner has been in the works for months. Every attendee has deep pockets and a demonstrated commitment the arts, but each one has to be convinced that this is a world-class institution that deserves expanded facilities designed by a top architect. We need to *compel* them to contribute." He paused.

"I fully agree, George. I'm primed to talk about education and visitor engagement," Jeremy interjected. Arthur smirked slightly when George ignored him.

"The gala needs to go off without a hitch."

"I'm sure it will," said Arthur, his voice admirably calm. He personally thought siphoning money from tonight's crowd would be easy compared to what he had to do to get Barbara to loan four paintings to his exhibition.

But George wasn't having it.

"This is supposed to be an exclusive event, and you two maniacs have planned a nudist show and some ridiculous kids' thing on the exact same night. How the hell did that happen? I want them cancelled."

"Cancelled?" cried Arthur and Jeremy in unison, looking at each other, then at John, who had moved to stand near George, his arms folded in solidarity.

"I can't cancel the tour, George," said Arthur, his anxiety mounting precipitously. "Not again. We'll upset the family irrevocably if we cancel with such short notice. We'll stay upstairs, completely out of the way of the gala."

"It's your job to be there, Arthur. Attendance is mandatory for all curators."

"I will be there, George, after I do my part of the tour. I'll get there in time for dinner. After all, I'm sitting with the Ramsays and they're aware of that," Arthur said. "Jeremy has the rest of the tour covered. Don't you?" He turned to Jeremy, who shifted in his chair again. The fact that "covered" was not the most appropriate word for a situation involving naturists escaped all four men at this tense moment.

"I thought you just said you were primed to talk up education," barked George. "Are you attending the gala or not?"

"Yes, I am, with my in-laws." Jeremy spoke rapidly. "You'll want to meet them—"

"Arthur's apparently figured out how to be in two places at once. How are you going to do it?"

"Actually, Rachel Burns will lead the second part of the tour."

This was news to Arthur. Jeremy had promised to handle the rest of the tour, and he'd assumed that meant he'd be leading it personally. But, of course, he weaseled his way out of the job and landed Rachel with it. That choice did not bother Arthur; he had every confidence in her ability, but he was surprised that Jeremy had not informed him.

Jeremy, oblivious to Arthur's momentary alarm, babbled away. "She's very competent. I knew you'd want me at the gala to represent education and visitor engagement. I know there'll be people there interested in sponsoring a—"

"Make sure she knows to stay upstairs," George interrupted. "Now, that kids' program. Cancel it."

Jeremy gulped. "TAG Camp is a really innovative new program. We've got twelve children registered. It's made for a good sponsorship."

"Did you not hear me? I said cancel it."

"Cancel it? We c-can't," stammered Jeremy. "We've had kids signed up for months. Some of them belong to board members," he added. Arthur noticed with some pleasure how Jeremy's customary confidence had vanished. If he wanted to impress the director, he'd have to stop fidgeting with his tie and start convincing George the camp would make him look good.

"Really? Board members?" George glanced at John, who nodded. "What'll these kids be doing?"

"They'll be mainly downstairs in the activity rooms," said Jeremy, who seemed to Arthur to be breathing a little easier. "The family programs coordinator has lined up a super program with a short tour. Just upstairs, of course," he quickly added as he saw George's face tense. "In the contemporary galleries. And marketing arranged for television coverage. They'll film the kids as they arrive and some of the activities. It'll show how innovative we are. It'll be good press."

"Um, George, do you still need me?" asked Arthur. His mind had drifted back to the Ramsay exhibition. He would much prefer to spend the day on organizational details than getting shouted at in George's office. He was already mentally approving the list of colleagues who should receive copies of the catalogue and he made a note to confirm the Ramsay works' arrival time with the exhibitions head. Plus he still had to write a proposal for the acquisitions committee and review a painting's restoration procedure with the head of conservation. Other tasks did not simply stop in the lead-up to a new exhibition.

"Yes," George bellowed. He strode around to his chair and sat, then looked at the three men with a disgusted expression. At that moment, his personal assistant opened the door and looked in.

"Excuse me, George, but they're here to get the drawings."

"Okay," he snapped. Two men from the special events staff called out "good morning" as they walked to the table.

"Would you like us to get that fixed?" asked one, pointing to the model. Relieved by the break, Arthur and Jeremy turned to see what they meant and noticed the rubble for the first time. They avoided each other's eyes as George growled, "Not now."

While the men quickly packed the architectural drawings in a large portfolio, Arthur contemplated with disdain the photograph of George glad-handing some rock star or other. His uneasy relationship with the director stemmed from knowing that George cared more for temporary exhibitions that drew high attendance figures, publicity, and huge donations than the ongoing collection-building and scholarly research that Arthur regarded as the core of curating. That fact that last year's presumed blockbuster, *Monet's Moments,* had failed to meet the projected revenue targets was a source of some comfort to Arthur. George conveyed satisfaction with the results publicly, especially to the board, but Arthur suspected that he desperately wanted that moment to pass.

Once the drawings were gone and the door closed again, George delivered his parting words. "Believe it or not, your first priority is to make me look good tonight. Focus on that."

Don't I always? thought Arthur wearily. He'd already polished George's aura by landing the Ramsay exhibition and keeping the donors placated. But he held his tongue. Jeremy was less cautious.

"Absolutely," Jeremy gushed, leaning forward. "I respect your vision, George. And I know exactly who I need to speak to tonight. When they hear about the visitor engagement centre…"

"Just keep your damn programs from interfering with my gala."

CHAPTER 7
RACHEL

"Find Naomi," Jeremy snapped at the departmental assistant.

Rachel looked up from her computer when she heard him give the curt direction. He rapped sharply on her door.

"You're here. I need to see you." He disappeared into his office.

Rachel sighed and took another sip of coffee before following him. She had arrived at work forty-five minutes late, hungover, and tired, hoping for a quiet, undemanding day before she went home to an early night. After a stop in the café to buy a cup of coffee, she entered the education area to see that Jeremy's office was empty. The receptionist told her he had been called to see the director. Indifferent to the reason for that meeting, Rachel concentrated on finding some aspirins, which she just managed to swallow before her acting boss barked his impatient command.

What does he want now? she wondered. Her head hurt. She clipped her TAG identity badge to her jacket, picked up her coffee, and walked next door.

"Good morning, Jeremy."

He nodded at his guest chair and she sat. She watched with perverse amusement as he brushed his light-brown hair off his forehead, undid the top button of his stylish blue-and-black shirt, and loosened his tie. She'd never seen him so discomposed and wondered what could possibly have happened during the meeting with the director to leave him so shaken.

Then Naomi Rosenberg, the coordinator of family programs, bounced into the room. In her late twenties, Naomi sported long, curly brown hair, a perky freckled face, and a multi-patterned dressing style that Rachel knew she could never pull off. Not that she'd want to; Naomi's jean jacket, black-and-white dotted tunic, and red-and-black striped leggings seemed to amplify her brash self-confidence. Her persona rubbed Rachel the wrong way, but sometimes she felt a bit corporate by comparison in her serviceable black pantsuit and white top. However, in her delicate state this morning, she needed the security her outfit provided. She wondered what Jeremy could want with both of them, as she had nothing to do with Naomi's area.

"Hi, Jeremy. You need to see me?" Naomi bobbed into the other chair and glanced at Rachel, then turned back to their boss. Jeremy had been instrumental in hiring Naomi, which ensured her admiring attention and an annoying sense of entitlement. He usually lit up when she appeared, but now Rachel thought his smile looked a little forced.

"Hi. Everything ready for tonight?"

"Yeah, I was just doing the setup. It's gonna be great," she gushed, tossing her curls. "Like, Melissa's going to love it." Jeremy's eight-year-old daughter had often attended the gallery's Sunday afternoon family programs.

"Wait a minute. Is that this sleepover thing? Don't tell me that's tonight too?" Rachel asked, sloshing her coffee as she jerked forward in surprise.

"This sleepover thing is called TAG Camp," snapped Naomi.

"It's not called Paintings and PJs anymore? Too bad," said Rachel sarcastically. "Wasn't it scheduled for next month?"

"TAG Camp fits the gallery brand better," said Jeremy. "Security has to work late for the gala, and the upstairs galleries have to be open for Barbara Ramsay's tour, so it made sense to schedule it tonight. That's why I called you both in. I want to make sure you're coordinated."

Rachel raised her eyebrows at Jeremy, wondering what meeting she'd missed. "Tour? Coordinated? What are you talking about?"

"Rachel, you know what I'm talking about," Jeremy said with an exaggerated sigh, removing a fleck of lint from his shirt and flicking it into his wastebasket. "The VIP tour for Barbara Ramsay and her group. She's a major patron. Arthur's doing the Canadian galleries and he needs you to take over in the contemporary galleries for the last half hour. It's all upstairs, out of the way of the gala."

A faint bell rang in Rachel's slowly reviving brain. Arthur's exhibition, due to open in a month, had stimulated a flurry of planning within the department, from Jeremy's video and audioguide to her lectures and panel discussions to the studio's watercolour classes. She vaguely recalled hearing that a family member, who owned four paintings, demanded a special condition for lending them. Now if only she could remember the condition...

"Wait a minute!" exclaimed Rachel. "The naked yogis?" At a meeting months ago, Jeremy had told his colleagues of this unusual patron request and they'd all tittered at the prospect.

"They prefer to be called naturists," said Jeremy. "It's Barbara Ramsay's yoga group. She demanded a guided tour for them and it's happening this evening. Obviously, we couldn't do it when the gallery is open."

"How can this be happening? What kind of coordination do you call it when a kids' thing and a naturist tour happen on the same evening? With a gala!"

"Look, Rachel, I'm sorry if this doesn't suit your need for crossing every 't' and dotting every 'i,' but that's just too bad. This is a very important tour, and I need you to do it. Donor relations are crucial," said Jeremy, folding his arms.

Gosh, Rachel thought. Stinger sounded more like the director every day.

"What do you mean, you need me to do it? I didn't know anything about having to give this tour!" In spite of her determination to keep her cool with Stinger, to not let him rattle her, she felt rattled. Did she have to take her clothes off? Where would she clip her badge?

"Impossible. You are the adult programs coordinator. It doesn't get more adult than this. Besides, I told you about it ages ago."

"You did not! I'm sorry, but I can't do it. I have plans for tonight. I think it's a professional courtesy to be asked to work overtime like this in advance, not to have it sprung on me at the last minute." Take that, Stinger! Carolyn's parting words echoed in her brain as she vowed not to bail him out again. Her only scenario for the evening entailed no alcohol and a good sleep, but Jeremy didn't have to know that. Let him squirm.

Eyes bulging, he threw his arms up in the air. "What do you mean, you have plans? You should have kept this night free. I need you to do this. You know that I can't."

"Why not?"

"I have to attend the gala. There'll be potential sponsors there. It's the perfect opportunity to tell them about my visitor engagement centre." *That damn visitor engagement centre*, thought Rachel. It wasn't even a sure thing in the expansion project. She stifled her opinion of Jeremy's obsession to pursue her resistance to his demand.

"Then why didn't you ask me when you first heard about it? Or when you knew you'd be unavailable?" Rachel folded her arms.

"Rachel, do you always have to be so anal? Do you know how much I have to handle in this job?" Jeremy ran his fingers through his hair. Rachel knew this was the closest he would come to admitting he had forgotten, or neglected, to notify her. "Of course, I asked you. This is a very important request. I would never let that slip through the cracks. I'm surprised you did, Rachel. You're usually so organized." Rachel kept her face neutral, although inwardly she flinched. She'd heard that dismissive tone before, when Stinger threw himself into his projects, claiming he needed creative focus for the big picture and expecting others to take care of administrative details.

"Yes, I am organized, which means I'd better get back to what I was doing. I'm sure you could leave the gala for half an hour to do the tour, Jeremy." She didn't like the fact that Naomi was smiling her faux-innocent smile.

"Don't tell me you're afraid of a little nudity, Rachel," Naomi sneered. It figured she'd take Jeremy's side yet again.

"Look, this gala is extremely important for the gallery's future," said Jeremy. "It's happening downstairs. Your programs are upstairs. Avoid the ground floor. Naomi, what time is the children's tour?"

"Seven thirty to eight. We're looking at the contemporary sculpture."

"Good. So, you'll be down the hallway from the Canadian galleries. Arthur will still be talking to the naturist group in there. You'll be back downstairs when Rachel takes them into the contemporary area at eight."

"If it's so important for the kids to avoid the naturists, why don't you do your tour earlier? Say six thirty to seven? Then you'll be back downstairs in the activity room and out of the way," Rachel said. "Remember what happened last November?" She had organized a guest curator's tour of an exhibition on a Sunday afternoon, only to find Naomi and a large group of children and parents encamped in the middle of it, creating tableaux, complete with costumes and sound effects, based on the paintings. Rachel still gritted her teeth when she recalled how Naomi had blithely carried on for a few minutes before cluing into Rachel's not-so-subtle glares and leading the group away.

"Oh, do we have to rehash that again? Like, get over it, Rachel. I've planned this program very carefully," Naomi pouted. "I can't just flip things around. The tour works better after they make their sculptures. I want to stick with seven thirty to eight."

"Well, if you're sure about that," said Jeremy. "You have to get them into that elevator by eight." He cast an anxious look at Rachel, who did not try to mask her disdain.

"Jeremy, like, I'm always ready to help you," gushed Naomi. "I can get one of my part-timers to do the VIP tour, if Rachel won't."

"Uh, thanks, but no, Naomi. I'd like a full-time staff person to handle this, which is why Rachel is doing it." Rachel glared at him, feeling miffed by the younger educator's offer to help him out, annoyed by Jeremy's continuing assumption that she would comply, but also sensing his desperation. The situation called for an experienced person.

"George is excited that we're piloting an innovative children's program. I told him you'd arranged for TV coverage," Jeremy continued, looking at Naomi. "Of course, I'll be available to speak to them at five thirty."

"Do you have time? Like, I'm sure I can handle it."

I bet you can, thought Rachel. Naomi and Jeremy were both always ready for a close-up.

"I'll make time," said Jeremy firmly. "Besides, I want to see Melissa and her cousin arrive."

"George is okay with all this?" asked Rachel. Knowing how the gala had preoccupied development and special events for weeks, she couldn't believe that the director had agreed to such a breach of exclusivity.

"Yes, he is," snapped Jeremy. "And I need you two to be aware of that. Your timing has to be perfect. Kids back in the activity room by eight. The naturist tour doesn't cross the hallway until they've gone. Access by the elevators. Nothing reaches the ground floor."

"Sure thing," said Naomi, with a hair-flip. *If she's not bouncing, she's flipping*, thought Rachel, sipping the last of her coffee. "Can I go now, Jeremy? I've still got lots to do."

"Okay. Make sure your helpers know the schedule."

After Naomi pranced out, Rachel remained seated, her eyes fixed on Jeremy. Bailing him out now meant he could swan around with wealthy donors at the gala; on the other hand, she could see that the unusual confluence of events demanded some delicate logistics. She was good at logistics. And he was her boss. Jeremy appeared to be scanning some papers as he said, "So, it starts at seven. You'll accompany the group the whole time and take over from Arthur at eight, when he joins the dinner. They can remove their clothes in the small room next to the elevators. It's empty now." Jeremy raised his eyebrows as he finally made eye contact. "No, you and Arthur don't have to do likewise. Staff stay clothed. Any questions? You know what's in those galleries, don't you?"

"Of course I know what's in the galleries. It's my job, as you well know," snapped Rachel. "What a screw-up that this tour and the sleepover got booked for tonight. I can't believe that George and John allowed this to happen."

"Rachel, I don't have time to listen to your complaints about senior management. Especially as I can't believe that you forgot about this assignment. I assumed you were working out the details. It's bad enough that I have to supply your program ideas and sort out the mess you made with the summit budget, but at least I thought you could handle a tour. Isn't that a basic part of your job?" Rachel's face reddened and she dropped her jaw, too stunned to reply. "I assured George and Arthur that you would deliver."

"I always deliver," said Rachel. *How dare he say I forgot*, she thought. Despite her righteous indignation, she didn't see any way out. Refusing to lead this silly tour would just give Stinger another weapon in his twisted campaign to undermine her. So much for early to bed. "All right. I'll do it. I'll call Arthur to let him know."

"I'm sure Barbara Ramsay will appreciate having such an experienced tour guide," he said. Rachel noted the relief in his voice and decided to ignore the forced flattery.

"Jeremy, are you sure Naomi realizes how important your instructions are?"

"Of course she does. I have complete faith in her. And you. I know you both want to make … education look good." Rachel could have sworn Jeremy was about to say "me" before deciding in favour of team spirit. She left his office.

Back at her own desk, she tossed her cup in the wastebasket. How had this happened again? Jeremy made it sound as if she'd forgotten about a tour he'd never asked her to do. Assuming her reliability and deflecting her reproaches at the same time. And firing fake accusations: "It's bad enough that I have to supply your program ideas and sort out the mess you made with the summit budget." She fumed at his self-importance and condescension, wishing she could escape it. She took a deep breath, then called Arthur.

They reviewed the tour itinerary and Rachel assured him she'd whisk the participants back to their clothes and out the door by eight thirty.

"It's kind of crazy having this tour on the same night as the gala, but I guess we'll just have to grin and bear it," Arthur said.

"So will the naturists," Rachel joked. Arthur chuckled, which made her feel better about the whole thing. As she put the phone down, she thought that she'd probably hear a few more puns regarding her first naturist tour, especially from her husband, whom she called next to say she'd be home late. Nick didn't disappoint.

"When you get home, I want to hear the bare facts," he said.

"I've already heard that pun. You'd better work on some others."

"Will do. I'll butt out now."

Rachel still resented the fact that she'd saved Stinger yet again, but part of her was beginning to look forward to it. She had led hundreds of tours, but sunbathing on a topless beach a few times in her twenties constituted her connection with public nudity. She couldn't tell if the flutter in her stomach meant she could face food again, after her coffee-fuelled morning, or if she was apprehensive about mingling with a bunch of naked strangers. She just needed stay awake and corral the naturists for half an hour. Maybe she'd get a peek at the gala. How bad could it be?

CHAPTER 8
AMANDA

Amanda sipped her green tea and contemplated her bursting inbox. She had a lot to do before she left early to go home and change for the gala, but she was finding it hard to concentrate. Her anger at George's outrageous decision about the sculpture commission had kept her awake half the night, mixed with anticipation about what might happen this evening.

On the personal front, Amanda would have to summon her considerable poise when one particular guest arrived with his wife. Three years ago, annoyed at her husband's inconvenient attachment to his teaching position in Vancouver, Amanda had divorced him and moved to Toronto. Her first two years in this job were intense, familiarizing herself with the collection, developing exhibitions, and getting to know the city's art scene. Specifically, getting to know the developers, business people, financiers, lawyers, doctors, architects, cultural mavens, and trendsetters who collected contemporary art. Many of them were members of the gallery's Gold Leaf Circle, who paid fifteen thousand dollars annually for the privilege of attending exclusive events at TAG, which often included talks by curators like Amanda. That's how she had met Steven Katz, who ran a high-end residential property company and joined the Circle a year ago when he wanted to expand his collection.

"My wife's been the 'eye' so far," he had told Amanda over a glass of wine at that first event. "We've got blue-chip work from the fifties and sixties, but I'm getting more interested in contemporary art. That's why I joined the Circle — to learn more about it."

"That's refreshing to hear," said Amanda. "So many men in your position would just hire an art adviser. Saves time."

"Not my style. If I'm going to build a collection, I want to know what I'm doing. Really get into it. It's a good antidote to work."

"Well, if I can help at all, I'd be glad to," replied Amanda, looking up into his dark brown eyes. Those eyes became more familiar to her over the next few months, as, through meetings and dinners, she carefully nurtured Steven's interest in the west coast photo-based artists shown in a local gallery. They had celebrated his first purchase of one such work by tumbling into a passionate affair.

The way that Steven managed their discreet trysts told Amanda that he was used to such extramarital activity, but discretion suited her. Amanda felt she could handle a brief chat at the reception, but she couldn't fathom spending a whole dinner with her lover's wife, so she had ensured that the special events staff seated them at another table. She would have enough collectors at hers to keep her occupied.

On the professional front, she smiled as she recalled her phone call with Justin, the installation technician, yesterday. She would seek him out for an update today, but first she had to handle some of her emails. Damn, another one from Samantha about the Havilio label.

> Your label violates the museum education principles of word usage and length.

Amanda began to fume as she wondered what the hell that meant.

> As an advocate for the visitor, I must insist that my label be used.

Those educators have a lot of nerve! It must be that arrogant Jeremy who had put Samantha up to this. Amanda clenched her hair for a moment, glaring at her computer screen. Then she wrote:

As a curator, I'm an advocate for the object.
Contemporary works are best understood within a
rigorous theoretical framework. If you familiarized
yourself with some pertinent readings, your label might
be more appropriate. Our high exhibition standards at
TAG preclude the inclusion of such banal content. I
cannot approve your label.

She pressed send. Labels! She cursed the fact that they had
become the Armageddon of museum work. If educators weren't so
uppity, her life would be easier.

Glad to forget that irritating task, Amanda dialled Justin's
extension. When it went to voicemail, she assumed he was working
in the galleries and left her office. She liked to check on Simone's
current exhibition, *Gestes*, as it was technically demanding. Four
cameras, installed at different locations inside the gallery, filmed
those areas and fed through a computer to a projector and screen
located in a street-level window near the entrance. The projection
rotated among the nineteenth-century gallery on the first floor, the
landing of the main staircase, and two rooms on the second floor. One
of those displayed Brodeur's videos of dancers and the other showed
the contemporary sculpture gallery. Passersby were entranced by the
peek at TAG's interior — a solitary security guard looking at his
watch, or a bouncy school group, or chatting adults — as the
projection alternated among the four spaces. Amanda popped
outside to check that the scenes were changing as they should. To her
chagrin, the projection was stuck on the staircase landing.
Fortunately, she saw that Justin and another installation technician
were working there, so she trotted back inside the gallery and up the
stairs.

"Hi, Justin. *Gestes* needs some attention."

Justin and his colleague had just lifted a bronze bust of Susannah
Littlewood, TAG's founder, onto a marble pedestal. He turned to look
at Amanda.

"Hi. We just need a minute to finish this." His colleague bent
down to rummage in a toolbox on the floor.

"We can't have the projection freeze up. I'll walk out with you."

Justin and his colleague exchanged glances, something Amanda had often noticed when she interrupted their work to summon them to one of her galleries. It was unfortunate they didn't realize how contemporary works took priority. As the other technician headed for the computer room, Justin walked with Amanda out to the window where the screen still showed the landing. Justin hauled out his cell phone to confer with his colleague. While he waited for a reply, he grinned at Amanda and asked, "Like my T-shirt?" He pulled aside his plaid shirt to reveal a black T-shirt sporting a white outline of a maple leaf containing the words Support Canadian Artists Now. "It's my first design for the collective."

"Timely," said Amanda. *Thank goodness that so many of the technicians were artists*, she thought. They were meticulous with the works, but also militant about TAG's contemporary projects. She had wanted a private moment with Justin. "Perfect way to make a point. How's that coming along?"

"It's short notice, so most of us weren't free at six thirty. But I've got four who can be here by eight thirty and stay until it ends."

"Fantastic." She watched the image on the screen flick from the staircase to the sculpture gallery and back again. Justin frowned as he described that to his colleague. A moment later, the nineteenth-century room appeared, showing a tour group listening to a docent. "That looks right."

"Yeah, it usually doesn't take long."

"Thanks, Justin. For this and for tonight." Amanda left him muttering into his phone and re-entered the gallery. As she walked back to her office, she smiled to herself. She had looked forward to tonight's gala, confident that she could help the director's goal by gaining hefty pledges for the campaign. Now that George's vision unfortunately included awarding the sculpture commission to Daniel Reid, she still felt resolved to play her part, but also to stand up for her territory. Justin's collective promised to be very useful in that regard.

CHAPTER 9
RACHEL

After the shaky start caused by her late night, Rachel got a second wind in the afternoon as she prepared her tour of the contemporary galleries on the upper floor. She always enjoyed walking through the beautifully installed spaces ahead of time, reviewing the major points and deciding how she would pace her commentary and questions. Art was her nectar and Jeremy's stings faded as she focused again on what she loved. She knew she would miss TAG's collection if she left.

After eating a quick supper at her desk, Rachel saw it was just six o'clock. There was still plenty of time before her tour, but, sensing an anticipatory buzz permeating the walls, she felt too restless to stay in her office, so she indulged her curiosity about the TAG Camp program. Over the past few weeks, Naomi had worked hard on its many components, from ensuring a high ratio of supervisory staff and volunteers to ordering an adequate amount of kid-friendly food. Rachel had gathered all that from overheard chatter but still didn't know how she missed the fact that TAG Camp piloted tonight. Why Jeremy did not see the need for the whole department to be aware of each other's programs eluded her. It wouldn't happen if she were the head.

She knew the children had arrived thirty minutes ago, so headed to the family programs room, a short walk from the education offices. Giggles and chatter led her to an open doorway, from where she saw

Naomi, two of her part-time staff, and two volunteers serving pizza to twelve boys and girls seated at two tables. A television cameraman circled them, watched by a woman taking notes. Rachel smiled as she saw Tina Chen, her friend in the marketing and communications department, turn from the female reporter and walk toward her. Before they could speak, she had to step away from the doorway as Jeremy and his wife burst through.

"Hi," she said, avoiding eye contact. "How's it going?"

Jeremy's wife gave a perfunctory smile. "Hi, Rachel. It's going great. Melissa and her cousin are having a ball." She waved at two girls, about eight years old, who waved back and smiled while chewing their pizza.

"Did you find time to do an interview?" asked Rachel.

Jeremy eyed her uneasily, but then looked at the room as he replied, "Yes, I did. She actually asked some good questions, and I was able to say how innovative this is. Naomi'll be pleased."

"Oh, she didn't get to talk?"

"Better to have coverage of her in action," said Jeremy. "I can give the big picture. If you'll excuse us, I have to change for tonight."

"Of course. Hope you enjoy it."

"Don't mess this up, Rachel. Keep those groups apart," Jeremy said through gritted teeth, then he and his wife walked away.

Tina edged up beside Rachel. "Stinger giving you his usual vote of confidence?"

"Yeah. What are you doing here?" Rachel knew that Tina rarely worked past five because of her two small children.

"Someone had to bring the TV crew here. I said I could do it, as long as someone took over at six. Gary's supposed to be here now," said Tina, looking around with a frown. "Why are you here?"

"I got hauled into helping Arthur with a VIP tour. That's what Jeremy was reminding me of, in his charming way."

Tina's eyes widened. "Another tour tonight? This is going to be some gala. I've gotta run. Tell me about it on Monday."

Rachel watched Tina dash down the hallway, wishing that she could join her. With a sigh, she turned back to the room. The assistants now sat with the kids, eating pizza, while Naomi bobbed in front of the camera. The education offices had been unusually quiet that afternoon as Naomi and her team prepared one space for the girls and an adjacent activity room for the boys to sleep in with the male staff member. Rachel had not had a chance to reconnect with her since the morning, so she waved as Naomi turned from the reporter.

"Rachel?"

"Hi, Naomi. Just stopping by. Looks like it's going well."

"It's fabulous!" Naomi beamed. "Was there something you needed?"

"Just checking about the timing. Your tour is seven thirty to eight, right? And you'll be in the sculpture gallery? Remember what Jeremy said—"

"Of course I know what Jeremy said. We'll be gone by eight. The upper floor will be, like, all yours," she said briskly in between glances at the kids. "You and Arthur stick to your route and we'll stick to ours."

"How long will the cameraman be here?" asked Rachel. Naomi flipped her hair and walked to her team, calling over her shoulder, "As long as he needs to. Don't worry."

I guess I'm dismissed, thought Rachel as she started walking away. She knew that Naomi liked to impress Jeremy, so it was a safe bet that the TAG Camp group would adhere to the itinerary he'd enforced. She hoped.

She returned to the second floor, where three spacious galleries showed contemporary art. She walked into the first one, which held the core of *Gestes*. The guards had left the videos on for the evening. Rachel walked to the middle of the large room and looked at the swooping forms of dancers moving across the white walls, emitted by overhead digital projectors. The artist, Simone Brodeur, named the show to reflect the contrast between her choreographed videos and the random movements of TAG visitors. Hence, she had placed a camera in this gallery as well as the three other locations that all fed into the street-level projection outside. The cameras ran during the gallery's regular open hours, but when the gallery closed to the public, guards turned them off, and Rachel assumed they had done so tonight. She decided to check out the gala setup.

A tune wafting from Littlewood Court, location of the dinner, drew her across the wide hallway. She walked down one arm of the grand wooden staircase and stopped on the landing where the bust of Susannah Littlewood, the gallery's founder, perched on a maroon and black-veined marble pedestal. The bronze sculpture took pride of place in the space and presided over all the Court's activities. Rachel wondered what Miss Littlewood would think of tonight's event, not to mention the expansion that would erase most of the remaining garden. True, her elegant home had by then all but disappeared in previous renovations. The venerable lady might welcome the contributions of Toronto's elite to help the gallery grow. Then Rachel remembered why she herself had to work tonight and wondered what the founder would think of a naturist tour and a kids' sleepover. She hoped Miss Littlewood's descendants were broad-minded, although if everything went according to plan, they would never find out.

The piano music pulled her from contemplating the bust to looking at Littlewood Court, a square, neo-Classical, two-storey space at the heart of the original gallery. White-painted stone piers and arches created a colonnade surrounding the marble floor. Along three sides, passageways led to the European rooms, which were designed in the same traditional style and featured high ceilings and impressive mouldings. At the second-storey level of the colonnade, a mezzanine embraced the Court on all four sides, allowing visitors to walk from the Canadian galleries to the opposite temporary exhibition spaces, or out to the second-floor hallway. Reaching from pier to pier under each arch, a trellis-like pattern of cast-iron vines formed railings as high as an adult's chest, providing a safe barrier for those who wanted to gaze down on Littlewood Court.

Rachel descended the six steps from the landing to the central arch. She gasped. She'd always admired the Court's day-to-day austere elegance, the rhythm of the arches, the outdoor light filtering through the peaked glass roof onto the gray-veined white marble and white piers. But tonight it was transformed.

Round tables, adorned with silvery-gray silky cloths over white linen and elaborate settings for eight people, filled the Court floor. Complex centrepieces of white roses and greenery sat in the middle of each table, surrounded by white votive candles waiting to be lit. Already the Court assumed a magical atmosphere, with the twilight above and tiny lights twinkling through the huge floral displays on tables fronting every pier. On the opposite side, a temporary stage held a pianist at one end and a podium at the other. To Rachel's surprise, eight dancers in pale-coloured leotards flitted off the stage and through the colonnade to the nearby elevator. They must be part of the gala. The scurrying special events staff looked too harried to ask. When a man who had been watching the dancers from a nearby arch turned toward her, she recognized the wire-rimmed glasses and neat dark beard of Simon Kinsella, the *Tribune*'s arts reporter. Rachel had never been interviewed by Simon, but had met him at openings and events. As she wondered what he was doing here, he approached her.

"Did you see that? It's going to be a fabulous performance," he said. She felt uneasy, given his well-known bent for poking at TAG's weak spots.

"Uh, no, I just saw them leave. What brings you here, Simon?"

"I'm covering the Avalon Dance Company. They're debuting a new dance they created just for this gala. Their director's a friend. She wanted an article on it."

"So you'll be at the gala?" Rachel asked, wondering how George would feel about Simon's presence.

"Well, at the edges. I'm not really attending the gala, but I've got to hang around until they perform." Simon gave a wry smile. "I know I'm not your director's favourite reporter, but I'm focusing on the dance. See ya." He headed toward the elevators.

Rachel forced a clipped smile and watched him go. Relieved that he had not asked her why she was there, she assumed he had no knowledge of what would shortly be happening on the second floor. But she couldn't shake an anxious feeling about Simon Kinsella's presence, tonight of all nights.

"Excuse me." A development staff person brushed by her, holding a tray of name cards. Six thirty-five. People were arriving, stopping to admire the Court, then continuing on to the reception. Rachel joined the flow, sensing their excitement as they greeted each other.

The sculpture hall, one of the suite of original galleries, was not as transformed as Littlewood Court, but it still looked impressive, with similar flowers adorning tall cocktail tables. She recognized the tune "Days of Wine and Roses" coming from her left and turned to see a jazz trio playing with the self-contained air of professional background musicians, creating a protective bubble in which to cast their spell. She moved a little closer to them to hear the music better but discreetly stayed at the edge of the crowd. Wait staff circulated with glasses of champagne and appetizers. People bent over the large model presiding in the centre of the room or studied the architectural drawings on easels along the far wall. George cast a curious glance her way, then returned his attention to greeting people with Victor. Roger and Amanda stood near the model, pointing and explaining. Rachel recognized some people from past gallery receptions and assumed they were long-time supporters, perhaps also on the board or active in the Gold Leaf Circle, the highest-level members' group. They all seemed to know each other and looked with keen interest at the model and drawings.

She noticed Jeremy turning away from a stylish-looking couple. Didn't take him long to buttonhole someone. It was now six forty. She'd better get moving. She couldn't resist walking by the jazz trio and smiling as they finished the tune, eliciting a nod from the pianist. They soldiered on through "Take Five," ignored by the chattering crowd, as Jeremy appeared in front of her.

"Don't you have a tour to do?"

"On my way." *You condescending bastard,* she thought. Her boss slithered back into the throng, while Rachel headed through Littlewood Court to the gallery entrance, stifling another yawn. She hoped Arthur would be in top form tonight. He'd keep her awake.

When she entered the front lobby, she saw Arthur standing near a few casually dressed adults. They contrasted with the late-arriving gala attendees showing their invitations to the development staff.

"Hi, Arthur. I didn't realize you'd be wearing a tuxedo. I feel underdressed."

"Oh, hi, Rachel. Don't worry, I suspect you'll be feeling over-dressed very soon," he said in an aside, nodding his head toward the growing group of naturists. "This isn't my favourite outfit, believe me, but duty calls."

Rachel smiled. "This tour kind of lends itself to all sorts of jokes, doesn't it? It must be one of your more unusual donor requests."

"The most unusual, without a doubt," said Arthur with a slight grimace. "But I've known Barbara for a long time and, if I'm being honest, it doesn't totally surprise me. It's just a bit inconvenient, tonight…"

"Arthur! Don't you look elegant!" A beautiful, slim woman wearing an expensive-looking sapphire-blue cocktail dress and stiletto heels extended her cheek for a kiss from Arthur. Rachel thought she detected heightened colour in Arthur's cheeks and wondered what this woman meant to him.

"Hello, Barbara. Meet my colleague Rachel, who's helping me with the tour."

"Fabulous!" exclaimed Barbara, shooting a radiant smile toward Rachel. She quickly looked behind her, her hair swinging in a smooth, graceful arc. "And here's Damian, my partner-in-crime." She entwined her arm through that of a tall, lean, handsome man who looked exactly like he did yoga every day. Rachel sensed an erotic charge between Damian and Barbara and noticed Arthur's lips tighten.

As newcomers joined them after checking in with security, Rachel assessed her first group of naturists. They were more mixed than she expected, mostly in their forties and fifties, some younger, a few older, and of every shape, size, and colour. Their exuberant greetings and lively chatter told her they all knew each other and looked forward to the event. The security manager directed a guard, Kirk, to follow the group.

"Okay everyone, listen up," called out Damian, stilling the chatter. "Great to see you all for this cool event."

"Let's hope it's not too cool," said a man, setting off some chuckles.

"Right, man. I just want to thank Barbara, who made this tour happen. Thanks, Barbara." He kissed her cheek.

"Welcome everybody. Well, normally we all follow Damian in his excellent yoga classes, but tonight we're stretching our minds, thanks to my old friend here," said Barbara, smiling at Arthur. Their eyes locked for a moment, then Arthur gave a neutral smile to the group. "Here are our tour guides — Arthur Matlock and, uh, Michelle."

After a few words of welcome, an explanation of the restrictions caused by the gala, and a diplomatic correction of Rachel's name, Arthur led the group up to a small nook near the *Gestes* exhibition on the second floor, the designated change room for the event. The naturists immediately began removing clothes and hanging them on the rack brought from the cloakroom, and within minutes, Arthur, Rachel, and Kirk faced twenty-five men and women wearing only shoes and socks. Twenty-four — Barbara had replaced her high-heels with spa slip-ons, a classier look than the outdoor footwear that the others favoured. Only Damian's brown Blundstones somehow managed to seem as appropriate as Barbara's slippers, but then Rachel figured he'd look good in anything — or nothing.

"We'll start in the Canadian wing," announced Arthur, his gaze firmly fixed on their faces. The group followed him across the hallway and through some rooms before reaching the one holding the earliest Canadian works. The naturists exhibited an unselfconscious demeanour that relaxed Rachel as she took her place at the back. She suspected that Arthur felt the same, although Kirk, obviously coached in non-voyeur behaviour, looked a little tense.

While Arthur started talking, Rachel glanced at the painting to her right, a late eighteenth-century scene of a stormy lake with white-capped waves and a careening ship about to capsize. *Too bad Stinger wasn't on it*, she thought, indulging in more annoyance about her enforced obligation tonight. Then she tuned back into Arthur's commentary. In spite of the unconventional appearance of his listeners, she could tell he was surrendering again to his love of his subject.

CHAPTER 10
AMANDA

The gala, with its alcohol-fuelled, back-slapping, dress-comparing, income-estimating, and art-collecting rivalries, was in full swing. Its participants were oblivious to TAG's other two events: animated children making sculptures one floor below and the lower-keyed tour one floor above, in which the possibility of outfit-assessing didn't exist.

The jazz trio's valiant efforts disintegrated in the reverberation of a hundred voices against the walls of the crowded sculpture hall. The bartenders re-stocked the trays with filled champagne flutes. In the nearby restaurant kitchen, the junior chef maintained an assembly line of platters replete with smoked salmon canapés, bite-size spring rolls, blackened shrimp on avocado and cucumber slices, carrot roulades with herb goat cheese, and skewers of Manchego cheese and chorizo sausage. The waiters performed a precise dance, swerving around each other as they returned empty platters, left with full ones, and carefully navigated through the hungry throng. Weaving among the attendees, the gallery photographer enacted a whirl of his own, cajoling smiles, capturing unposed shots as they surveyed the model, and avoiding anyone momentarily in the unflattering, puff-cheeked action of chewing.

Amanda turned to face Steven and his wife.

"Amanda, hello," said Steven, his sharp eyes taking in her appearance approvingly. "I'd like you to meet my wife, Ellen."

Amanda smiled. Ellen's full lips, which Amanda assumed owed a lot to injections, twitched in an approximation of the gesture. "I gather you're the one who's been tutoring Steven," said Ellen. Amanda's stomach fluttered with discomfort. She suspected innuendo, but Ellen's next words reassured her. "He's enjoyed your talks so much. I can't believe how much our collection's changed."

"I'm glad you're getting used to it, Ellen," said Steven. "We couldn't just keep buying colourful abstracts."

"In my experience, collectors enjoy discovering new work," Amanda replied, relieved. She hoped she struck a diplomatic tone, not caring to hear any spousal disagreements on art. She watched Steven deftly take two glasses of champagne from a passing tray and hand one to his wife. He had checked that her glass was still half-full. "And their enthusiasm helps the gallery. We do appreciate it."

"Especially tonight, I bet. Cheers," said Steven, raising his glass. Over the rim, he caught Amanda's eye for a moment before he sipped. "So how much of this expansion is for contemporary art?"

"Let's get Dietrich to tell you," said Amanda, waving over the momentarily free architect. Ellen had listened to her politely, then scanned the room, as if looking for people she knew. Amanda was relieved at her lack of interest, but still felt a bit unnerved at meeting her lover's wife. A distraction would be useful. After introductions, Dietrich launched into his practiced pitch about the advantages of the expansion, focusing on the new and refurbished galleries, more attractive to potential campaign donors than mundane features like enlarged storage vaults.

"This foyer in the new wing," said Steven. "I've heard something about a major sculpture commission?" His eyes darted to Amanda, then back to Dietrich when she remained tight-lipped.

"That's right," said Dietrich. "It's a great space for a statement sculpture. Two storeys high. Glass walls. I think George may have an announcement about it tonight."

Damn, thought Amanda. If Dietrich knew about it, then George and that bloody Zach really *had* been scheming behind her back. She sensed Steven observing her closely, but she ignored him and plastered on a smile as Victor joined their group.

"Victor Drake," he said heartily, shaking Steven's hand. "I think I've seen you at our Gold Leaf talks." Amanda suppressed her urge to leave and finessed the introductions.

"Ambitious project," said Steven. "Dietrich's been filling us in. I gather you're the chair of the campaign?"

Victor raised his glass. "Yes, new turf for me, but I'm in the saddle. Looking forward to getting lots of people on board tonight."

Here we go, Amanda thought. Horses as usual, and now boats. At least he was expanding his vocabulary. But she refused to encourage him.

Luckily, she didn't have to; Dietrich took the bait and filled Steven in.

"Victor is donating a superb collection of British horse and hunting scenes to the gallery. They'll be the centrepiece of the new European rooms." A woman tapped his arm and Dietrich flowed into a new shoal of buoyant guests.

"I'm pleased that the European curator thinks my little group of paintings is worthy of this institution," said Victor with a smile — one that faded only slightly when Amanda hid a snort of derision with an unconvincing cough. Her reaction stemmed from the eureka moment she'd had earlier in the day: she remembered why the name "Hathaway" had rung a bell. That knowledge cast a pall on the chairman's donation, unbeknownst to him.

Victor ignored her and carried on. "They really knew how to paint horses back then. I look forward to seeing them in the rotunda. In fact, there's a drawing of it over there if you want to have a look." He gestured toward the array of architectural renderings across the room. "This expansion project is long overdue. The vaults are bursting. Gotta get that stuff out." *How poetic*, thought Amanda. Victor made it sound as if they were having a jumble sale.

"Giving them the pitch, Dad? Oh, hi, Amanda." Zachary Drake raised his glass of champagne at Amanda and smiled at his father. A young woman, attractive except for the bee-stung lips that distorted her face, clung to his arm. As Victor made introductions, Amanda cast an assessing eye over the man who had insinuated himself into her territory. She wondered what he'd promised George to get him to award the sculpture commission to a high-profile American artist. Or maybe George had manipulated Zach into gaining prestige through funding it. Perhaps Victor had made a deal. Whatever. It was a travesty, no matter how it came about.

Amanda had met Zach a few times at commercial gallery openings, but his image was more familiar from the fashion and events pages of the magazines that she leafed through at her hair salon. Taller than Victor, Zach shared his father's fleshy face and deep-set eyes, but his tan, blond-streaked collar-length hair and fashionable stubble presented an air of laid-back cool rather than the sharp focus of a business magnate. *Or, at least, that's what I assume he wants to project*, she thought, wondering if his girlfriend's skimpy dress came from Zach's ZAD line. She would stick with Holt Renfrew.

"As I was saying," said Victor, "the gallery really needs this expansion. Can we count on you?" He raised his thick eyebrows at Steven.

"We haven't had a chance to look closely at the model yet," said Steven. "Shall we, Ellen?"

"Yes, of course. Thanks for coming," said Victor, clapping Steven's shoulder as the couple moved away. Amanda, behind Ellen's back, gave Steven a clipped smile, which he returned. She hoped they would be able to find a moment together later in the evening, but now she turned back to Victor, Zach, and the restless-looking girlfriend.

"It'll be awesome to see a Reid sculpture in that new wing," said Zach, picking up a canapé from a passing tray. "It's about time Toronto had a piece by him. And the space to put it." Amanda was glad she had just swallowed her champagne, because she knew she would have choked again at Zach's easy assumption that she agreed with the choice of artist. Before she could reply, Victor squeezed his son's arm.

"I'm so glad you're becoming an art patron. Reid's work is not my taste, you know, but that big space needs something. Glad you made it happen. But I'd better mingle." With a brisk nod at the three of them, he bounded over to a nearby couple.

"Big night for Dad," said Zach, looking after his father. He turned back to Amanda. "Me too. About time I supported the arts. Did you know the dance performance tonight was my idea?"

"Uh, no. How wonderful."

"It was really cool meeting Daniel in New York," Zach continued, turning to his girlfriend.

"Daniel Reid's an important name," Amanda said. She couldn't dispute that. "The gallery's so fortunate to have generous supporters like you and your father." Again, truthful, if only said out of obligation.

"And now they're building this new wing for one of his works. Wouldn't have happened without me."

Amanda admired donors who espoused the gallery's mission as their own, but she thought less of those who decided to rewrite it. George would not take kindly to such self-aggrandizing statements either, and she wondered if the director would regret bringing Zach into the fold of high-end patrons. Amanda was beginning to feel she'd had enough of Zach Drake, and her heart sank further when the gallery photographer emerged from the crowd and urged the three of them to get closer. She forced a smile on her lips, noting with disdain the excitement of Zach's date at this diversion. As the photographer veered off, she decided to change the subject.

"Tell me how your business is going."

"Great! The summer line's selling well. It's terrific, as you can see." He gestured to his girlfriend's dress. "And I'm curating a series of fashion events at a club on Richmond. Music, clothes, booze. Should be awesome."

Amanda felt her smile tighten. Pretentious twit! The guy paid for one sculpture. Now he thought he was a curator? "How interesting," she said. "If you'll excuse me, I must follow your father's example and mingle. Enjoy the evening." She glided into the chattering crowd, grateful that Zach and his ZAD-wearing date would not be sitting at her table.

CHAPTER 11
GEORGE

George stood at the podium in Littlewood Court, waiting for the last of the guests to leave the reception and find their tables. Seven twenty-five. Right on schedule. He savoured the animated hum in the room — a result, he felt, of the excellent champagne and appetizers they'd just enjoyed and the thoughtful groupings of eight at each table in the exquisitely decorated Court. He had taken great care to ensure everyone was seated in congenial company, including Susannah O'Brien, the eighty-three-year-old great-niece and namesake of their founder, who was accompanied by her daughter and son-in-law. George had been pleased to notice them quizzing the architect about the expansion, but while he was accustomed to Mrs. O'Brien's keen interest in her great-aunt's legacy, he couldn't help but wish it came with more financial support. He strongly suspected the Littlewood fortune had dwindled over the decades. Mrs. O'Brien may not be able to contribute significantly to the building campaign, but it made for good relations to invite her to major gallery events.

Seven twenty-eight. George felt pleased with his curators. They'd mingled well at the reception and now looked comfortable with their well-chosen dinner companions. Roger and his partner, Pierre, enthralled their audience, no doubt recounting an anecdote from a trip.

At a nearby table, Amanda leaned toward a young couple whom George didn't recognize, but he assumed were new collectors. He had ignored the frosty look she had shot him at the reception, as he knew she would make the most of this chance to charm patrons. He frowned as he noticed two empty chairs at a table just beyond Amanda's. It was the Ramsays' table, and George realized that the other settings waited for his errant curator Arthur and that woman who had demanded the naturist tour. *A donor with such an outlandish request should cough up a healthy pledge in return*, he thought. Next to the Ramsays' table, he saw Jeremy and his wife. George had met her parents briefly and noted they seemed spellbound by their son-in-law's spiel about the visitor engagement centre. If they were prepared to give a sizable donation, maybe he could squeeze it in somewhere. But that was a consideration better left until later. It was time to deliver his speech. He nodded at the pianist, who stopped playing.

"Good evening and welcome," he said. People turned from their neighbours and leaned backward or forward to see him better. "I'm George Caldwell, director of the Toronto Art Gallery. Thank you all for coming and showing such generous support for our next phase.

"I hope you all had a good look at the model and the drawings. They show that we are about to embrace a new era. I have no doubt you are as inspired as we are by the potential of this expansion project and I know that we can make it happen, with your enlightened backing.

"Before we all enjoy another fantastic meal prepared by our renowned chef, I need your attention for a few minutes while we tell you about the new wing. I'll be joined in this by two crucial members of our team, Dietrich Becker, the architect, and Victor Drake, chairman of the board of trustees and chairman of the TAG21 campaign."

As George continued with the requisite remarks — thanking the government funders already pledged to the project, thanking the staff and others who had organized the event, briefly explaining the need for enlarged gallery and storage space that drove the expansion — he looked around the Court. Familiar with his text by now, he wanted to gauge the receptivity and attention of his audience. He knew many of the guests were prominent philanthropists, supporting theatre, dance, music, film, and the museum, accustomed to periodic events like this one to lure more tax-deductible cash from their hefty accounts. The collectors in the audience appreciated the rise in status conferred by the expansion, making their local gallery an attractive home for a future donation. The faces raised toward him expressed a range from polite interest to smiling encouragement. Confident that he'd set the tone, after exactly five minutes, he introduced Dietrich and took a seat beside Victor behind the podium.

"Well done. We're off to a good start," said Victor in a stage whisper. "I've lined up a few pledges." He folded his arms in satisfaction, then leaned closer to George, who tried not to flinch at the smell of smoked salmon and alcohol emanating from Victor's mouth. "How long do I have again?"

"Four minutes," said George, looking determinedly at Dietrich's back. They'd both heard his talk many times, a polished description of the new wing, the galleries, the interior renovations, the improvements to the front façade, but George resolved to pay attention so he knew exactly when to step up to the podium once more. Timing was crucial. The waiters stood poised to deliver the appetizers as soon as the remarks concluded. Victor knew that. George might have found his board chair's anxiety touching, if it wasn't such a pain in the ass.

As the applause followed Dietrich's speech, George vaulted back to the podium, repressing a wince as his sore knee objected to the move.

"Thank you, Dietrich. That was a wonderful description of the entrance to the new wing, a truly auspicious space to mark the transition from our elegant sculpture hall to the new European and contemporary galleries. We here at TAG think this is the perfect home for a newly commissioned sculpture. I'm very pleased to announce, here tonight, that we are giving that honour to leading American artist Daniel Reid. It will be his first commission in Toronto."

A ripple glided around Littlewood Court, mostly due to the more art-savvy guests smiling and nodding and murmuring approvingly. Those who didn't pay as much attention to contemporary art asked their neighbours why it was such a big deal. George kept his gaze away from Amanda.

"That exciting project is not the last impressive announcement tonight," he continued. "Please welcome our chairman of the board, and chairman of the TAG21 campaign, Victor Drake."

George glanced at his watch as he returned to his chair. Seven forty. Still on track.

"Thank you, thank you. Thank you so much for coming. I join George in thanking those who are already in harness with us as well as all who worked so hard to organize this wonderful evening. Dietrich's produced a beautiful design for us, which I hope will spur on many of you to pledge generously to support the expansion and help our great gallery become even more outstanding. We need people to stay the course as we head to the finish line. If I can use a bit of racing world jargon, heh-heh." Victor paused and looked up from his notes. George fixed his eyes on the chairman's broad back, as if compelling him to get on with it.

Victor grabbed both sides of the podium. "I know many of you collect art. It's a passion. My first passion, which I indulged once my business became successful, is horse breeding. One of my thoroughbreds ran in the Queen's Plate last year. This love of horses led to my second obsession — collecting paintings of horses. Horses at the hunt, horses at rest, horses in races, but mostly at the hunt. Those of you who collect know that tracking down your next purchase can be an addictive sport." George noticed a glance pass between Roger and Amanda at the chairman's mention of his favourite topic. He hoped nobody picked up on their disdain. Yeah, Victor was a bore, but he'd like to see them produce a ten-million-dollar donor. He refocused his attention back on the chairman.

"It's my good fortune that my wife, Delia, has indulged me in this sport. But my time on the board here at TAG has made me realize the value of making great art accessible to the public, which is a bigger prize than keeping it in our home. So it's my honour to tell you that we'll be donating our collection of eighteenth- and nineteenth-century British paintings to the gallery, to be placed in the new

European wing when it opens. And to help that happy day come about, Delia and I are giving ten million dollars to the building campaign. I invite you all to join us in this exciting new venture." As the applause welled up, Victor nodded at his wife, who blew him a kiss from her seat just below him. George quickly strode to the podium, shook Victor's hand, and leaned in front of him toward the microphone.

"Thank you, Victor and Delia. We couldn't be more thrilled to have this extremely generous start to the campaign. We look forward to your support. Enjoy the dinner."

Applause surged up and the pianist resumed playing. People seated in the corner of the Court near the kitchen shifted to watch the line of servers, arms bearing plates of tantalizing crab salad, emerge from the colonnade and head briskly to their designated tables. From the other side of the Court, servers sprang up to fill glasses with the Chablis chosen for this course. Victor and George remained on the stage for a moment, their right hands still clasped, their left arms holding each other's right shoulders, suspended in mutual appreciation of the long-awaited moment as the gallery photographer leapt back into action to catch it. The launch of the campaign! Everything was proceeding as planned. How could the guests not share Victor's generosity and follow his lead? The director felt proud of his flushed and grinning chairman.

"Well done, Victor. Champion speech!" That was it for the horse racing references.

"Thanks, George. Glad that's over. But I think I sold 'em." He released George's hand and lowered his other arm as he turned to smile at the crowd, a few of whom raised their newly filled glasses in appreciation as they caught his eye. "Looks like I didn't need to bug you about all the arrangements so much after all. It's going swell."

CHAPTER 12
ARTHUR

"Do you have any paintings of nudes in this gallery?" A female naturist interrupted Arthur's talk on a rugged landscape.

One of her colleagues retorted, "We'll have to suffice for now."

Arthur smiled along with everyone, then said, "Actually, we do. That's our next stop." He led them into the Salon, where three teal walls displayed paintings from ceiling to floor, in a collage of landscapes, portraits, scenes of nineteenth-century daily life, townscapes, and a few nudes. The large room served as the gateway to the Canadian wing and opened to the hallway. Diagonally opposite from that entrance, an archway led to the mezzanine overlooking Littlewood Court. Kirk, their security guard, moved to stand in front of that opening, to Arthur's relief. Best to keep this group corralled, not that they had behaved disruptively so far. They continued to listen with absorption as he explained the academic training that drew several artists of the time to Paris.

When Arthur ushered them further into a corner away from the hallway, he heard young, excited voices filter in from that direction. *Must be those kids*, he thought. *It's only seven thirty?* Glancing surreptitiously at his watch, he saw it was seven forty-five. Hmmm.

His mind shot back to the meeting in George's office that morning. They were supposed to be much farther down the hallway by now. He noticed Rachel shoot him an anxious look, then dart out of the Salon.

"Arthur?" Barbara spoke softly. She looked at him with a slight smile and raised eyebrows. He realized he must have paused longer than he meant to while registering the hallway sounds. He smiled back, keeping his eyes focused on her face, as he had throughout the tour. A nude Barbara in close proximity was potentially distracting enough; he didn't need unwanted action just outside the Salon. He rallied to focus on the remaining fifteen minutes of his tour.

"Ah, yes, here we have a few scenes of everyday life," he said with gusto, claiming the naturists' attention again. He had barely uttered one more sentence when he sensed two new disturbances, as if a secret force was ruffling the air. Kirk frowned and turned to look at the mezzanine. Arthur thought he heard an unusual noise from there but couldn't discern what it was, so he carried on with his explanation of innovations in painting, a subject he could recite in his sleep. To his dismay, a few of the naturists glanced toward the mezzanine, while others turned their heads toward the back of the group. Damian had left his position beside Barbara and assumed a yoga pose, standing on his left leg, with his right foot anchored on the inside of his left thigh, right knee bent out, arms upraised.

"Damian, what are you doing?" asked Barbara.

"The tree pose! What would you expect? All these landscapes. I couldn't resist," Damian said with a grin, dropping the pose and stretching his arms. "These spaces are great. We should have a yoga class here."

"We can discuss that another time," snapped Barbara. Arthur's heart leaped at her tone and irritated expression. "Sorry, Art. Please continue."

Tree pose? That yoga guru, or whatever he is, had a lot of nerve to mock my beloved collection, thought Arthur. He wondered what Barbara saw in him, a fleeting thought that mingled with his appreciation of her support and anxiety about what was happening on the mezzanine. Forget kids! Forget Damian! Taking inspiration from the magnificent works around him, whose creators never let mountains, forests, or indifferent society deter them from their artistic goals, he channelled the spirit of Canadian art and pointed to his last painting.

CHAPTER 13
RACHEL

Her heart thumping, Rachel shot out of the Salon to look for Naomi and the TAG Camp. She had repeatedly glanced at her watch for the last fifteen minutes, waiting to hear them emerge from the elevator and walk to the sculpture gallery down the hall, safely away from the naturists. But it was seven forty-five, she had to take over from Arthur soon, and they were late.

She looked to the left of the grand staircase, where the long hallway led to several galleries. Empty. To her horror, she heard noise from the right side of the staircase. She dashed to the opening to the mezzanine and stopped short, blocked by the TV cameraman. She couldn't believe what she saw over his shoulder. Twelve TAG campers, costumed in capes, dresses, and funny hats, stood along the east side of the mezzanine, laughing and brandishing flashlights as they looked over the railings down into Littlewood Court. No doubt their outfits and props were meant to add a sense of adventure to their sleepover, but Rachel didn't care about the creative aspect of Naomi's programming right now. She was more concerned about her supervisory ability. Where was she? And the rest of her team? The cameraman abruptly stepped onto Rachel's foot as he backed toward the hallway.

"Hey!" she hissed. "Watch out." She scurried out of his way as he ignored her, walking slowly backward and keeping his camera on the group. In the next few seconds, a harried-looking Naomi bounced from the mezzanine, herding six children in front of her. The other supervisors, looking equally stressed, appeared down the hallway with the other six in tow. With the kids momentarily silenced, Rachel heard noise wafting up from Littlewood Court: piano music abruptly stopped, crashing china, gasps, and cries. Oh no. She glared at Naomi.

"What are you doing? You're supposed to be there," Rachel snapped, pointing down the hallway. Naomi had a reputation for going off-piste, but this was ridiculous.

Naomi crouched to stage-whisper to her young charges: "Indoor voices. Go to them." She gestured to the rest of the camp. The kids headed in that direction, followed by the cameraman and reporter. Only then did she turn toward Rachel, with a look combining embarrassment and anger. Rachel had never seen the family programs coordinator look so shaken before. She would have enjoyed it if she wasn't so tense herself.

"Not now, Rachel. Like, we ran late, okay? Those TV people want to see everything."

"It's really important we keep the two groups apart," said Rachel. "I'm going to be taking the naturists into *Gestes* soon. You'd better be out of the way."

With a clipped "I know," Naomi pivoted and trotted toward the TAG Camp group, who turned left into the contemporary paintings gallery. Weren't they supposed to go into the next room? At least they were out of the way. Rachel took some deep breaths to calm herself and wondered if Naomi would remain Jeremy's favourite after this debacle. As the piano music resumed in the Court, her pounding heart slowed. She returned to the Salon, where the naturists seemed oblivious to the recent unscheduled activity so nearby.

CHAPTER 14
AMANDA

"Please excuse me," Amanda said as she rose from the table. "I'll just pop to the washroom to deal with this." Wine spilled on her new dress! At least it was white wine on a black dress, but still, not something she expected at a gala. The past few minutes had been a nightmare.

The drama began as George and Victor were about to end their moment of mutual appreciation on the stage. Amanda's tablemates stopped their chatter about the Reid commission as a woman's scream rent the air. Looking in that direction, Amanda saw a young waitress, open-mouthed, staring at Susannah O'Brien's chest, which now held her crab salad. Another waiter deftly straightened his arm to save two plates from a similar fate, but his less nimble colleague sent his exquisitely plated cargo crashing to the marble floor.

The other wait staff froze, heads turned upward. Amanda followed their gazes. The mezzanine around the upper level of Littlewood Court, which should have been empty, contained undeniable signs of life. Some kids hung over the railings while a few adults strove to yank them back. Mystified as to why they were there, Amanda looked back to the stage, where George stared at the kids with a thunderous expression. As the distracted pianist abandoned "Fly Me to the Moon," she thought that George probably would like to board that flight right now.

Her momentary contemplation of the director's distress ended as one of her tablemates, twisting to look up at the kids, knocked her wine glass over. Skeptical comments halted her attempt to escape to the washroom to clean up.

"What was that all about, Amanda?" asked a man facing her. "Seems an unusual approach to fundraising."

"Unusual is right. I wonder about the administration of this gallery if they let children wander around during an exclusive event," said his wife.

Another man commented, "I'm surprised that Victor would allow it. When I bumped into him last week, he boasted about how he'd been helping George organize this shindig. If this is his idea of taking the reins, to use his favoured terminology, I don't see how he's going to build a new wing."

"Let Amanda go. She needs to deal with her dress," said his wife. Amanda threw a grateful smile in her direction and strode to the nearby washroom. A few minutes later, picking shredded paper towel off the front of her dress, she emerged to see Steven Katz leaving the nearby men's washroom. He brandished his tuxedo-covered left arm at her. It looked wet.

"Oh, no, Steve, what happened?"

"Some salad flew up when the waiter dropped a plate. Hit my sleeve," he said with a shrug. "It'll come out." He smiled wryly. Amanda glanced around. The hallway was empty. She nodded toward the nineteenth-century gallery and they slipped in there. He held her shoulders and kissed her. Then Amanda stiffened and stepped back. After all, this was her workplace.

"Not here," she whispered.

With a wry smile, Steven raised his hands and shrugged. "Quite the night."

"Do you mean the unexpected guests or George's announcement?"

Steven laughed. "Both, I guess. Where did those kids come from?"

"Don't ask me," said Amanda. "Education's always up to something. I've no idea why they appeared. It's just another example of George's pathetic organization. In case you were wondering, I also had no idea that Daniel Reid was going to get that commission. Until yesterday." She folded her arms and tossed her head, unable to meet Steven's eyes. He took a step closer and stroked her arm.

"I thought there was something bothering you at the reception. I was shocked when he said that name. Didn't you mention some female artist to me?"

"Yes. Simone Brodeur." Amanda now regretted having mentioned anything about the commission. It had just come out, the way things do in a post-coital chat. "I shouldn't have told you. And I certainly shouldn't have said anything to her. But I thought it was my decision to make, not the bloody director's."

"Right. What can you do about it?"

"I'm not sure. Announcing it tonight is a big deal. I feel like George has run roughshod over me."

"Has he learned that from Victor?" At Amanda's quizzical look, Steven added, "His horses." She snickered.

"We heard more than we needed to about them tonight, didn't we? No, George had domineering tendencies before Victor arrived, but he's never done anything this bad before." Amanda recalled the papers she'd seen on George's desk during that awful meeting. "But maybe you can help me."

"Sure. How?"

"George and Victor seem awfully close, and now Zach is involved. I'm pretty sure he's funding the commission."

"Really? I didn't think his company was that successful."

"I'm sure it only keeps going because Daddy lets him pay a lower rent in his malls. Anyway, George and Victor. It's natural they're so close, given they're both so hot about the new wing, but I wonder if something else is going on. You're in business. I don't know how much your circle overlaps with Victor, but could you do a little investigating for me?"

Steven raised his eyebrows. "About what?"

"Just about Victor's business, how he runs it. Anything shady? Any scandals?"

"What do you suspect?"

"I don't know yet, but I've got a hunch. Something to do with an appraiser named Hathaway. If you can find out anything in the business arena, I'd love to know."

"I know a few people who know him better than I do, so yes, I guess I can do that." Steven stroked her arm again. "Look, babe, I'm sorry this happened. I'll do what I can. But I'd better get back there now." He nodded toward Littlewood Court.

Amanda waited a minute so they would not be seen leaving at the same time. She felt that Steven would help her on the Hathaway front, just as she assumed Justin was helping her on the Reid front. Then she was distracted from her battlefield musings by a sensation of being watched and turned to see Simon Kinsella looking at her from the other end of the gallery. They knew each other professionally, as he had often interviewed her about contemporary exhibitions.

"Hi, Amanda. How are you enjoying this glittering affair?" he asked, walking toward her.

Amanda stood her ground, swallowing hard. Affair? Strange word for Simon to use. Then she decided it had nothing to do with Steven and herself. The gala. Simon couldn't possibly be an attendee. He wasn't even wearing a tux.

"Hello, Simon. What brings you here? Is the *Tribune* covering the gala?"

"No, I want to cover the dance performance. It's a world premiere, you know."

"Oh, right." Amanda remembered the schedule. "That's at eight thirty, isn't it?"

"Yes. You should get back to your table so you can enjoy your meal before it." He glanced at the lower part of her dress and she self-consciously flicked at an imaginary miniscule ball of shredded paper towel. "I don't think you got any salad. Those kids caused a bit of a stir."

Amanda smiled tightly, fearing it might look more like a grimace. That was all TAG needed, a gala going off the rails and a reporter who loved pointing out gallery fuck-ups. She avoided Simon's eyes and wondered how much he had seen of her chat with Steven. Who else was going to pop up at this damn event? She chose to ignore his barbed comment and take the high road so she could escape.

"I'm looking forward to the performance and to your review. Good night, Simon." She sensed his amused expression as she strode away.

CHAPTER 15
ARTHUR

"Thank you for your attention. I'm sorry to leave you, but as I said, duty calls, and I must attend the gala downstairs. I'll turn things over to my colleague Rachel, who will take you through some of our contemporary galleries." While acknowledging the naturists' applause with a smile, Arthur looked at Barbara.

"I'm sorry that I have to say bye to you too," she said, "but I'm expected to join Arthur and my family at this dinner. Enjoy the rest of the tour."

As Rachel led the group into *Gestes*, Arthur and Barbara walked to the nook where she could retrieve her clothes. Arthur stood just outside while she did so, but in earshot of Barbara.

"Your friend Damian seems very, um, spontaneous," said Arthur. He still felt miffed about the unexpected display of athletic balance and six-pack abs that Damian had contributed to the tour, but also reassured by Barbara's annoyed response. "Is he always inclined to take on a yoga pose at the drop of a hat?"

"We all dropped more than a hat tonight," said Barbara, smiling as she emerged, dressed and shoving her spa slippers into her bag. Feeling relieved that his gentlemanly self-enforced avoidance of looking at her naked body had ended, Arthur allowed himself a moment of appreciation. Barbara looked beautiful.

Arthur smiled back. "Barbara, you look very nice."

She arched her eyebrows. "Easier to say that now I'm dressed? Thanks, Art. How sweet of you. I've never seen you in a tux before. Very smart. And thanks for being such a trooper about my request. You'll get your paintings. Is—"

"Thank you!" Arthur interrupted her, not his usual style, but he was thrilled to hear Barbara say it at last. He quickly kissed her cheek, then she stepped back and asked, "Is there a place I can freshen up?"

He pointed out the nearby woman's washroom, then stood in the hallway, holding her coat as he waited. During the tour, Barbara had remained on the edge of the group, out of his view; whether that was a considerate act on her part, or a desire to stay near the unpredictable Damian, he didn't know. He felt a mix of relief that the loan was secured and pleasure at her compliment.

The murmur of conversation, clinking glasses, and music rising from Littlewood Court broke into his thoughts. Apparently, the gala was proceeding as planned, in spite of the mysterious noise on the mezzanine. If anything had disturbed George's precious event, he'd have to brace himself for another embarrassing attack. He sighed and hoped Rachel could get the naturists safely out of the gallery in the next twenty-five minutes.

"Are we late?" asked Barbara, snapping him out of his reverie.

"No, we're right on time. They've just served the entrée. Let's go this way," he said, guiding her toward the elevator.

As they entered, Barbara said, "Damian's not my friend, you know." At his surprised expression, she continued, "You called him that a moment ago. Sure, we dated for a while, but I've found out he's a little too fond of other female students. Younger ones." She shrugged. "Easy come, easy go. He was fun in Hawaii when I met him, and I arranged this tour for him, but I never expected that he'd be so rude. Interrupting your fascinating talk by showing off his yoga pose! I think it's time to move on."

"You arranged this tour for *him*?" Arthur asked as they stepped out onto the main floor. He felt touched by Barbara's unexpected confession, although it was hard to imagine her being cast aside by anyone. What was wrong with that Damian? The yoga world must be harsher than he thought.

"Oh, he's always urging us to find venues that will accept naturists," said Barbara, stopping in the hallway. "I didn't do it just for him. I thought it would be great. And any chance to bug Dad and Alex. You know they thought this tour was a crazy idea."

"You've been bugging them for a long time," Arthur said with a smile. He knew they should be heading into Littlewood Court now, but he felt intrigued by Barbara's revelations.

"I'm sure Alex has told you all sorts of stuff about me. Including that I'm a terrible mother."

Arthur gulped. This was sensitive territory. Alex had indeed told him that Barbara's twelve-year-old daughter, Lily, had been sent to a boarding school out of town at the insistence of her ex-husband. Apparently he felt their daughter was better off seeing as little of her mercurial mother as possible. However, Arthur did not feel up to judging anyone's maternal qualities and merely murmured empathetically. Barbara bit her lower lip, as if to hold back tears. She looked at him.

"I probably am. Or have been. But I want to change. I want to have a good relationship before she turns into a teenager. If I can. Time to stop chasing New Age follies."

Arthur thought that confining her naturism to private yoga classes was probably a good place to start, but Barbara's forlorn expression kept him from a tart retort. He opted for a benign connection that had just occurred to him.

"My only connection with New Age follies is a crystal my niece gave me. By the way, she's the same age as Lily." Relieved to see Barbara smile, he placed his hand on her elbow and nodded toward the Court. "I want to hear more about her, but we really should get in there now." They started crossing the hallway. Arthur stopped a gala staffer and asked her to bring Barbara's coat to the cloakroom.

They wound their way through the tables to where the Ramsays sat in the middle of the Court. Barbara seemed to shake off her seriousness with a toss of her hair and sashayed along, apparently oblivious to the admiring glances a few men gave her. Following in her wake, Arthur realized her free-spiritedness had made him dismiss her for years. She couldn't possibly be serious or interested in him. Now he wasn't so sure.

Alastair, Margaret, Alex, and his wife stopped eating their grilled chicken for a moment to greet them. Wait staff materialized instantly with plates and wine. Arthur took a quick gulp. What a night.

"Are all your galas this lively, Art?" asked Alex, with a twinkle in his eye.

"Uh, lively? What do you mean?" Arthur's stomach flipped and he put down his knife and fork.

"There was a disturbance a while ago, just after the speeches," said Margaret. "Some children appeared up there." She nodded toward a corner of the mezzanine. "They weren't there long, but they surprised us all."

"Children? What are children doing here at night?" asked Barbara, shooting Arthur a sharp look over the rim of her wine glass. "Good thing they didn't bump into our exclusive tour, Art."

Arthur gulped. "It's an education thing. They're sleeping here overnight. The mezzanine was supposed to be off-limits. What happened?"

"A few waiters lost their focus," said Alex. "Some plates went flying, some wine got spilled. We were okay."

"Susannah didn't fare so well," said Margaret, nodding her head in the direction of Mrs. O'Brien. Arthur remembered that they were old friends, and cast a surreptitious glance at Mrs. O'Brien, whose chest bore a big wet stain. Although she seemed to be enjoying her entrée now, Arthur knew he'd be hearing from her. She was not only the founder's great-niece, with a robust interest in everything at TAG, but also a strong supporter of his department through the Littlewood Fund for Canadian Art. He may not be as smooth a schmoozer as George Caldwell, but he knew he had to keep this patron on his side.

"It was definitely an odd thing to happen at a fundraiser, but it didn't last long," said Alastair. With a stern glance at his daughter, he added, "I'm relieved it wasn't your group up there. That would have been a bit too much for a father to bear."

"Bare's the word, Dad," said Alex. Everyone laughed while Alastair shook his head. At that moment, the photographer, pleased to see new subjects, broke into their conversation and asked them to look his way.

"Oh, relax, everyone," said Barbara after the photo op. "Our tour went off without a hitch. Art was brilliant. He sailed through it as if it was all in a day's work."

"As if you'd know what a day's work is, Sis," said Alex. Arthur used to silently agree with his old friend's jibes at his carefree sister, but his recent conversation with Barbara had changed things. He felt more protective of her now, so he assumed a neutral smile. "And I trust Art's finally earned your paintings. Let's drink a toast to that." As everyone raised their glasses, Margaret placed her hand over Barbara's.

"I'm so glad you've agreed to lend your works too, dear. It makes the exhibition even more special for us to have the whole family involved."

Barbara looked at her mother in surprise. "Of course, Mom."

Arthur realized that Margaret had derailed her daughter from a sniping comeback and thought Barbara looked touched. He smiled in acknowledgement of the toast and sipped some wine.

"Tell me about this new wing," said Barbara. "I take it someone's going to ask me to contribute?"

"I think Art needs a moment to eat," said Margaret. "But the director told us all about it."

I bet he did, thought Arthur, cutting a slice of chicken. He hadn't felt hungry when they sat down, given the events of the night, but he knew he should eat, if only because the waiter was already refilling his wine glass. He settled into comfortable conversation with these old friends, flattered by Barbara's admiration for the Canadian galleries and her questions about the exhibition preparation. Far too soon for him, the background music stopped, and they all looked at the stage, where George had returned to the podium.

"Now that you've enjoyed a delicious entrée, without any surprises … we'd like to whet your appetites with an enticing interlude before your desserts arrive. The Avalon Dance Company has choreographed a short dance, called *Generosity*, in honour of our TAG21 campaign, and if you'll direct your attention to the grand staircase, we'll be treated to it now."

"How wonderful. I love dance," said Barbara. "What a lovely event, Art."

Arthur smiled absent-mindedly, having forgotten that a dance was part of the gala schedule, but appreciative of Barbara's enthusiasm. They all shifted in their chairs to face the east side of the Court, where a spotlight lit the grand staircase and the bronze of Susannah Littlewood on the landing. He had recently requested that the bust be cleaned and he allowed himself a moment of curatorial pride as he observed its fresh glow. He hoped that the impressive view of this monument to her great-aunt would mollify any discontent felt by Mrs. O'Brien at the earlier mishap. In a moment of collegial solidarity, he glanced to the mezzanine above, noting that Rachel was somewhere behind it, about to end the tour, which he hoped had proceeded discreetly. As the pianist changed to more strident music, he obeyed George's instruction and focused on the grand staircase.

CHAPTER 16
RACHEL AND GEORGE

Two events workers quickly slid the podium to the side to make way for the dancers as George stepped down from the stage. Damn! His knee flared up again. He winced, hoping nobody noticed. His chair already faced the east side of Littlewood Court and the grand staircase, so he did not have to shift as his tablemates were doing. He allowed himself a gulp of wine. The last introduction done. Maybe he could relax now — that is, relax as much as the gala allowed. After all, it was a fundraiser and George still had to buttonhole some likely donors. His circulation at the reception had yielded a few pledges, but he knew there were more generous veins to mine in this crowd. Get through this dance, then dessert, then he could mingle again. Courtesy of the well-stocked bar in the sculpture hall, the last phase would provide a perfect opportunity to chat up more potential donors.

As long as they aren't pissed off by those damn kids appearing on the mezzanine, he thought ruefully, taking another swig of wine. George had received a few disgusted looks from those who hadn't dodged the falling plates or spilling beverages. He could only hope that the replacement salads and the succulent entrée had achieved the desired soothing effect. He could use a little soothing himself, but his glass was empty. As he looked around to catch a waiter's eye, he sensed a change in the Court's atmosphere that had nothing to do with the strident piano music accompanying the dancers. He tensed. What now?

***

In the ten minutes she spent talking in the *Gestes* exhibition, which was softly lit by the flickering videos, Rachel found her footing with the naturists. It helped that her listeners' nudity — their range of large and small breasts, fit to sagging midriffs, hairy or scrawny chests, faded tans, and bare crotches — was less obvious in the dim gallery. Although Damian, perhaps inspired by the images of cavorting dancers, had struck a contorted-looking pose at the back of the group, Rachel was gratified that only a few naturists noticed him. The group moved without mishap to the next gallery to look at contemporary paintings. She assumed that the campers must have left by the far elevator by now and decided she had just enough time for a short stop in the contemporary sculpture room next door before wrapping up.

When she led the group to the opening to the hallway, Rachel expected to see the same quiet space that she had walked through a few minutes before. She froze. It was filled with activity. From the elevator to the right, eight dancers flitted toward the grand staircase. She realized it must be time for the performance that Simon had told her about. At least they were adults and focused on their work. Then, she became aware of chatter to her left, emanating from the group of children and adults who, for some unaccountable reason, were just leaving the sculpture gallery. As the dancers split into two groups to stand at each wing of the staircase, the naturists bunched up behind Rachel became restless.

"Why aren't we moving?"

"Who are they? Dancers?"

"Damian, check this out!"

Then Rachel heard more voices from the end of the hallway.

"Look at the bare-naked people!"

"Gross!"

"I wanna dance too!"

To Rachel's horror, the kids started running toward the staircase. Some seemed determined to follow the dancers, others wanted to gawk at the naturists. As the music in Littlewood Court changed, the dancers began descending the stairs, their normally poised expressions appearing strained, as if they wanted to escape this floor to the relative safety of the stage below. Rachel felt like a puppet on a string, as she yanked her head from one side to the other: she wanted to run to the staircase to stop the kids and stay here to keep the naturists back. Years of art history classes, training docents, wrangling speakers, all her hard-won experience disintegrated in the face of wayward small people and irritated naked people. The latter became more vocal:

"What are those kids doing here?"

"I thought we had an exclusive tour!"

Only Damian seemed unperturbed by the new arrivals in the hallway. He strolled over to the railing to watch the dancers descend, copying their swaying arms as he did so. Rachel started to run toward him to tell him to rejoin the group, when she was distracted by loud voices to her left. Kirk had slipped by her to confront Naomi. He pointed to the left elevator.

"Take your group down that way!" he snapped. "Get them out of here."

"You go that way," cried Naomi, gesturing to her team members who had corralled four of the kids at the head of the staircase. "I'll get the others." Rachel saw her fly to the left wing of the staircase, red-faced. Her helpers mustered the children toward the left elevator, not an easy task as they kept turning back to look at the naturists, some of whom had fanned out from behind Rachel to join Damian at the railing.

"Why don't they have any clothes on?"

"Look at their bums!"

***

The dancers had left the stairs and were tripping lightly along the sides of the Court toward the stage, but George saw unexpected action behind them. Those bloody kids again!

"Fuck!" The expletive escaped from him in a hiss, but he realized from his wife's grip on his arm that it was louder than was appropriate for the director of one of the city's leading cultural institutions. George stared in horror as several randomly costumed kids galloped down one branch of the staircase and the remaining steps. Three adults tailed them but failed to catch up before the kids barrelled into the Court, slamming into tables and blinding guests with their waving flashlights. A little girl cried out, "Hi, Mommy, we're gonna be on TV!"

Another exclaimed, "We're dancing!" Jeremy sprang up from his table and grabbed the two girls by their wrists, pulling them into the colonnade on the left. The adults reached the other six kids, who'd been blocked by a guard on the right. Almost as soon as they'd arrived, the kids were whisked away. *Good riddance*, thought George. Noticing the shaking heads of the shocked guests, very few of whom were watching the performance on the stage behind him, he regretted that he'd agreed to let this damn camp happen tonight. George vowed to give Jeremy a piece of his mind. He noticed a couple at the back get up. Strange time to go to the washroom. Oh no, they headed for the entrance. Out of the corner of his eye, he caught Arthur leaning toward a stunning woman who must be that wacko donor who wanted the nudist tour. Naturists. At least they were keeping out of the way.

***

Rachel noticed that the cameraman and reporter evaded Kirk, who was propelling the kids and supervisors toward the left elevator. A naturist behind her exclaimed, "Hey, what's that camera guy doing here?"

She stepped forward to ask the TV crew to leave, but new sounds directed her attention back to the grand staircase. At first she could not discern what was happening, as the lineup of naturists along the railing blocked her view. Although the piano music in Littlewood Court continued, there seemed to be more vocal sounds than you'd expect from well-heeled adults watching a performance. Cries. Gasps.

"Look at Damian!" exclaimed one of the naturists at the railing. The remainder of the group behind her pushed forward toward the staircase. Rachel dashed to the right side to see what was happening. She froze.

On the landing, Damian had assumed the dancer pose. He stood on his left leg and extended his right hand to hold his upraised right ankle, neatly framing the bust of Susannah Littlewood with his arm, bent leg, back, and buttocks.

Rachel forgot about the TV crew or that the naturists would not know where to go next. All she could think of was getting Damian out of the view of Littlewood Court. She ran down the steps to the landing.

"What are you doing? You have to stay with the group."

With an annoyed expression, possibly due to her blocking the spotlight, Damian lost his balance for a moment and grabbed Miss Littlewood's bust with his free hand. To Rachel's horror, the bronze sculpture, which should have been securely bolted to the pedestal, began to lift toward Damian. Which would be worse — the distinguished likeness of their founder tumbling down the stairs to land at the feet of an astonished gala patron, or the undistinguished reality of this yoga guru doing the same? On the brightly lit landing, in front of one hundred distracted diners, with the photographer rushing toward the staircase, Rachel unceremoniously yanked Miss Littlewood back. Damian swayed toward the opposite stairs, then righted himself.

"Cool it, Rachel. You should try yoga sometime," he called over his shoulder as he nonchalantly ascended. As she watched him for a second, Rachel caught Kirk returning to place his hand over the cameraman's lens and usher the TV crew away. She rested her hands on the bust to make sure it sat safely in place. Sorry, Miss Littlewood. She shouldn't be touching her without white gloves, but this was an emergency. Thank goodness the *Gestes* camera on the landing would not be on tonight.

"Good catch, Rachel."

Abandoning her tender moment with TAG's founder, Rachel turned to her left. Horror struck again. The naturists had obediently followed her down to the landing. Shit! They're giving the gala another show. Face reddening, she scampered up the opposite stairs, the naturists plodding behind her.

***

George reached for his empty glass and again tried to catch a waiter's eye. However, all the wait staff had joined most of the guests in continuing to look back toward the staircase instead of at the stage. What the fuck? George kept that outburst to himself as he registered the tableau on the landing. A naked man held an absurd pose in front of the bust of his gallery's vaunted founder. An escaped naturist had penetrated the elegant splendour of his gala! Then a woman in black appeared to tussle with him. What the hell was going on? Where was security?

George looked wildly back at the stage. The dancers carried on. But people at the next table were pushing their chairs back. They cast disdainful looks in George's direction, not bothering to lower their voices as they said, "Some gala this is. The museum's fundraiser went like a charm. They know how to run an event."

"I'm not inclined to give to a place where I get my food tossed onto my lap and a nudist show."

To George's horror, all the people at that table rose and started walking out through the colonnade. Before he could stop them, he heard a loud cry to his right. He turned to see Susannah O'Brien, eyes closed, leaning against her son-in-law. Christ. The old bat had fainted. He couldn't help thinking that it wasn't a bad way to escape this mess, but his growing fury eclipsed his concern for an ailing patron. With a clenched jaw, he looked back at the staircase, where the spotlight technician, no doubt confused by the additional performer, had kept the light on the landing, which now displayed a line of naturists crossing it to ascend the opposite stairs. Fuck! The photographer, torn between the action at two ends of the Court, again taxed his pivoting skills to capture both.

***

Rachel reached the top of the stairs and took a deep breath. What had just happened? She had never been in such an absurd position, arguing with a naked man in front of a hundred people and saving a bronze bust from toppling down the stairs. At least the hallway appeared to be back to normal. Kirk and the TV crew were just disappearing into the elevator. Not completely normal: Near the entrance to the sculpture room, Damian struck the warrior pose.

CHAPTER 17
GEORGE

Out of the corner of his eye, George saw Arthur look with alarm at the reclining Mrs. O'Brien as a staffer scuttled over in a half-crouch to help. *You'd better take care of her*, he thought. *It's your damn nudists who helped create this disaster.* He leapt up to dash to the south colonnade, ignoring his wife's perplexed expression. More people were leaving! If he couldn't stop them, he could at least make sure that the development staff gave them the campaign packages. Damn! There were no staff at the tables lining the colonnade; they had gathered in an archway to watch the dance, not expecting to encounter departing guests until much later. George grabbed a package, waved it at the startled employees, and pushed it in the face of a well-known business executive. The man stopped, placed his fingers on one corner of the envelope as if it were contaminated, and looked at George scornfully.

"Was that appalling show supposed to be performance art, George? I'm not sure that people bursting into a gala with no clothes on is a good theme for fundraising. Implies you want to take the shirts off our backs to pay for your new wing!" His wife huffed in agreement and they marched off. *Shit*, thought George, momentarily lost for words. Well, at least they took a package. Relieved to see that the staffers had stopped watching the ongoing dance and were back at the tables, but dismayed at the number of guests who were leaving, George ran his fingers through his hair and whirled around to face the Court. Victor shot him an angry look but then turned back to the dance. As he figured he would not have to face the chairman's ire for a few more minutes, George took a deep breath. How was he going to save this fucking mess? Not all the tables were emptying; he saw the Ramsays, Jeremy and his companions, and Mrs. O'Brien and her group were still seated. Amanda and Roger looked as if they were treading water, struggling to keep their tablemates focused on the dance.

Then he heard a stage whisper beside him: "Lively gala, Mr. Caldwell." With a sinking heart, George turned to see his nemesis, Simon Kinsella, approaching with notebook in hand.

"What the hell are you doing here?" hissed George, abandoning everything he'd ever learned about media relations.

"I'm covering the Avalon Dance Company. They were really looking forward to the profile their new work would get from debuting here." Simon, also keeping his voice low, nodded toward the stage. "But they seem to have some competition. Care to comment?"

George glared at him. Of all the creeps to show up tonight. As he saw Simon's expression change from smirking to alarmed, he realized that his own must look thunderous. Good! Let the bastard sweat. The reporter stepped back a pace, but rallied his journalistic chops for another dig.

"I know that TAG wants to broaden its audience. Does this mix of programs indicate a new direction to that end?" At that moment, the piano music swelled up as the dance ended. The smattering of applause saved George from a reply as Simon turned to watch the dancers take a short bow. They split into two groups again, apparently planning to leave the Court by their entrance route, but stopped in confusion as the departing guests blocked their way. A quick-witted events staffer ran on to the stage and led them off in another direction.

George saw Victor get up and braced himself for his next confrontation. "No comment," he barked, sending Simon off to follow the dancers. As George moved toward the sculpture hall, for more privacy, he almost bumped into a waiter emerging from the kitchen, arms laden with dessert plates.

"Excuse me," snapped the waiter, swerving around George and heading steadfastly toward the emptying Court. The next one in line asked, "Hey, where is everybody?" But George ignored that as he slunk between them, then marched to the main entrance of the sculpture hall. As if compensating for the diminishing chatter in the Court and reading the temperature of the room, the pianist swung into a robust version of "Stormy Weather."

"George! Stop walking away from me! What the hell is going on with your gala?"

George sighed and turned to face Victor, who looked like he was going to explode. *Your gala. So much for all our months of mutual planning*, George thought. But he wasn't surprised that the chairman had reverted to his favourite tactic when TAG went awry.

"I wasn't walking away from you. I wanted to get to a more private place," said George, more calmly than he felt. "Let's talk here." He stepped just inside the sculpture hall but still in view of the Court and, unfortunately, the wait staff restocking the bar for the post-dessert phase of the gala.

"This is outrageous," fumed Victor. "What kind of a place do you run? I came here tonight to announce my donation and I get nudists and kids running around. Someone had the gall to say to me, 'I knew you were into horseflesh, but I didn't think we were going to see so much human flesh!'" He stopped when George snickered in spite of himself.

"Think that's funny, do you? I don't know about you, George, but I take my responsibilities bloody seriously. I'm proud to be the chair of the board and the chair of the building campaign. And I'm ready to do my share of arm-twisting to squeeze some loot out of these hoity-toity saps, or at least I was. But your gallery is a bloody circus!"

George winced at the phrase "hoity-toity saps," thinking it did not bode well for Victor's fundraising technique. *Your gallery is a bloody circus.* That's truer than he wanted to admit.

But he didn't need Victor rubbing it in at this moment.

"Look Victor," he said, placing a hand on the other man's shoulder in what he hoped was a reassuring manner. "Your speech was fantastic. But I don't have time to argue with you now about a few, um, unexpected events. There are still people here. Let's go get some pledges."

Victor looked at him as if he'd lost his mind.

"Pledges! What the hell do you expect me to do? Run after them and pin them in a half nelson? Nobody in their right mind would donate to this nuthouse!"

"You're still the chair of the TAG21 campaign and I need your support," said George through gritted teeth. "I'll thank you not to denigrate the gallery anymore. You should be talking it up, not chewing me out."

At that point, Victor's wife appeared around the corner and led him to a nearby table, where the guests sat, restless but still captive. George, moving toward the Court, saw that the chairman seemed to summon his schmoozing skills for one last charge. The room was still half-full with guests chewing in a half-hearted manner and looking around at the uneaten tiramisu and Grand Marnier souffles on the empty tables. With an unerring sense of what was most needed at that moment, the resolute pianist embarked on the classic ballad "People."

Red-faced, George stood for a moment, looking at the Court, taking a deep breath to recover from Victor's attack. He spied a couple to whom he had not yet spoken and began walking toward them across the marble floor, disregarding the cross and curious looks sent his way by Mrs. O'Brien's daughter and others. But then something happened that he couldn't ignore: He slid on some crab salad that was missed in the earlier clean-up and collapsed onto his sore knee.

"Christ!" he shouted, eliciting more disdainful looks. He leant on a table as he painfully struggled upright, then grabbed a napkin to wipe salad from his trouser leg. The couple whom he'd been aiming for moved a step away. The man asked, "If you think going down on bended knee will get a donation, you'd better think again, George. We don't expect nudists and children at a fundraising gala."

"Was that performance art, George?" his wife asked in a sneering tone.

How many times would he have to hear that attempt at art-savvy humour? George hid his irritation and cajoled the couple into joining his wife and the rest of his table in the sculpture hall. Victor's and Jeremy's tables headed that way too. But the sight of Arthur and Jeremy reignited George's anger about the mishaps and he decided to abandon fundraising for the greater satisfaction of telling them off. He nodded to them to follow him and strode into the nineteenth-century gallery that ran alongside the Court, out of view of the stragglers.

"Congratulations, George," Jeremy said, a bit breathlessly as he scurried to catch up. "What a great evening. I've met some—"

"Shut the fuck up!" snarled George. Jeremy recoiled and shot a look at Arthur, who morosely contemplated their boss. "What is the matter with you two? I gave you strict instructions to keep your damn groups out of the way, and away from each other, and what happens? The kids suddenly appeared on the mezzanine. As if that wasn't bad enough, they ran into the Court. And those damn nudists put on a show on the landing! Precisely where I said they should not be. What part of that did you not understand?"

"I understood it perfectly," said Jeremy. "And conveyed it clearly to Rachel and Naomi. I don't—"

"Maybe you need to assess your staff's abilities," snapped George. "Christ. Victor had just finished his big announcement, a very important one for the gallery, and the place turns into a bloody circus!"

"It didn't last that long," gulped Jeremy. "I'm sure that most people—"

"Long enough," said George. He looked at Arthur without any hope of reassurance. "Well?"

"I'm sorry that things went awry for a moment or two," said Arthur, "but how bad can it be? Are people really going to not contribute to the campaign because of a bit of nudity?"

"Yes," shouted George, making them jump. "And it wasn't just nudity. There were kids shouting at people. And then running around the tables." Jeremy winced. "It makes us look like we can't organize our way out of a paper bag, let alone run a building campaign. I've had to listen to questions about my management, how we supervise kids, what kind of programs we run. And of all the people to get her food dumped on her, one of them had to be Susannah O'Brien! She isn't likely to cough up. Christ." George pivoted away from them, running a hand through his hair.

Jeremy took a deep breath. "Arthur has a point," he said. "Torontonians are enlightened. They know we need this expansion. And the visitor engagement centre. I'm sure Victor's speech inspired them."

George looked at him with contempt, wondering how this chattering twit got the nerve to keep bringing up his damn visitor thing. "I'll have a hell of a mess to clear up on Monday."

"I'll investigate this right away. And I'm sure I've found some sponsors," said Jeremy.

George glared at him. "I don't give a fuck right now, Jeremy. I'll deal with you on Monday." Jeremy blanched and sped out of the gallery through the far entrance. George turned toward Arthur. They faced each other at right angles to the other entrance.

"You know, we wouldn't be in this mess if you didn't have to do that fucking tour," he shouted, causing Arthur to flinch. "What kind of a ditzy donor needs to bring her bloody nudist friends here anyway? She should be glad that her paintings are getting a prestigious venue like ours. So should her parents. We shouldn't have to jump through hoops to get a bunch of dingy old landscapes."

"If they're such a burden for you to show, maybe we should approach another gallery."

This time it was George's turn to gulp, as he slowly turned to see a group of people standing just inside the entrance. The Ramsays! A beautiful woman in a blue dress approached him, hands on her hips, apparently the one who had spoken. George realized with dismay that she must be Barbara.

"Barbara, so sorry you heard that. George didn't mean it. This evening's had some, ahh, complications," Arthur sputtered, edging out of George's orbit toward his friends. "So sorry," he repeated, daring to glance at Alastair and Margaret. They looked stunned.

Barbara ignored him and glared at George. "It dawned on me that our group might have caused some trouble by appearing on the staircase. You shouldn't blame Art; our leader is a bit too spontaneous. I came here to apologize on his behalf, so you wouldn't be upset with Art. But maybe you'd rather we took our dingy old landscapes elsewhere."

"No, no, not at all," said George. "I'm terribly sorry, Barbara. You caught me at a bad moment. We've had some problems here tonight. My stress got the better of me. Arthur knows that, don't you?" George looked anxiously at him.

"Of course I do," said Arthur, with a slight smile, as if savouring the director's embarrassment.

"We came here to see if you wanted to join us for a drink, Art," said Alex, "even though things seem to be winding down," he added with a scornful look at George. "But maybe it's time to leave."

"A drink! Great idea," said Arthur, taking Barbara's arm by the elbow. "Let's get over this unfortunate slip."

"I could use one," said Barbara, slowly removing her steely look from George, "but I don't feel like calming down."

"I'm truly sorry," George said, forcing a smile. "We look forward to seeing your works here in a month."

"We'll see about that," called Barbara over her shoulder. They left.

George stood for a moment, running his hand through his hair. What the fuck had just happened? As if the night wasn't already a disaster, he had just made it worse by insulting lenders. He didn't know whether to go to the sculpture hall and get plastered or find another employee to harangue. At that moment, one of the security guards entered the gallery.

"What the hell are you doing here?" spat George.

"We just found out those *Gestes* cameras are still on. I have to turn them off." He headed for the barely visible door that gave access to the camera's controls.

"Christ!" yelled George. "That's all we need." He collapsed onto a bench, rubbing his knee. He quickly withdrew his hand in disgust, glaring at a spot of salad dressing.

CHAPTER 18
RACHEL

Rachel had wrapped up the tour at eight forty. A woman fell into step with her as they walked back to the nook containing the clothes.

"Thank you so much. I don't usually like contemporary art, but you really helped me to see there's something to it." She chattered on about how wonderful it must be to work at TAG, while Rachel struggled to appear interested. *TAG's appeal as a workplace has definitely declined tonight*, she thought. She just wanted to get these people out of here and go home.

In the main lobby, the naturists stopped to thank her.

"I think TAG offered some new insights on events management tonight," said Damian. "But thanks again, Rachel. We all enjoyed it. Right?"

"Except for that TV camera," said a bearded man. "I hope that guard took care of it."

"I'll look into it right now," said Rachel, noticing a huddle of guards at the desk.

"Chill out, man," said Damian. "Normally I'd say do some yoga, but there's a good pub down the street. Let's go for a drink."

Rachel breathed a sigh of relief as they left. For a moment she stood watching them, unable to move. How did this night turn out so badly? The collision with the TAG Camp kids, the excruciating scene on the landing. Had Jeremy seen it? *There'll be hell to pay on Monday*, she thought and felt reassured that she had started an escape route. The university art gallery job looked even better now.

She squared her shoulders, calm enough now to speak to the guards about the cameraman's filming. She walked over to the security desk, where Kirk, the guard who had escorted her tour, stood with his colleagues, sharing some appetizers from a nearly empty platter. One of them slid it toward her.

"Did the kitchen take pity on you?" she asked, taking a spring roll. "I'm glad that's over. Thanks for getting rid of that cameraman, Kirk. Did he film the naturists at all?"

Instead of answering, Kirk raised his arm triumphantly toward Rachel and cried, "And the TAG award for courage above and beyond the call of duty goes to Rachel Burns!" The other three guards clapped.

Rachel stared at him, uncomprehending, until he nodded his head toward the lobby's far side and said, "Nifty move with Miss Littlewood."

She followed his gaze to the huge glass wall that showed the main floor hallway and the grand staircase. Between the doors leading to the hallway, the landing and branching stairways were clearly visible. Her face reddening, she quickly chewed her spring roll, then made a mock bow.

"Oh, you guys, it was nothing! You would have done the same."

The guards laughed.

Kirk said, "To answer your question, yes, he had a few minutes of your naturists but he deleted it, after some persuasion. That's why I was here when they appeared on the landing. When Miss Littlewood almost went flying, I figured I'd better get back upstairs."

Rachel winced at the phrase "your naturists," then shook her head. "I'd like to know why that bust wasn't securely bolted. The installation guys shouldn't let that happen."

"Right. What a night," muttered Kirk, taking the last cheese and sausage skewer from the platter.

"Hey man, look on the bright side," said another guard. "You got to ogle a bunch of nudists. Makes a break from looking at the same old art."

"Ogling wasn't part of the job," said Kirk. "The boss was pretty firm on that."

"At least the *Gestes* cameras weren't on. No chance of my tussle with the bust showing up outside."

"Uh, I'm afraid not, Rachel," said the guard who'd been at the desk all night. "We just noticed that people were gathered outside so we're turning them off now."

Rachel's eyes widened. Shit! Could this night get any crazier? If the cameras were on, then the naturists could have been filmed on the landing, in *Gestes*, and in the sculpture gallery! She was speechless.

"And there's some other group outside with signs," continued the guard. "They're peaceful so far, but we're watching them."

While Rachel listened to the guards recount the night's mishaps, she noticed a number of gala guests lining up at the cloakroom to get their coats. Oh dear! The event was supposed to go on until ten thirty and it was only nine. She shuddered at the thought that the kids and naturists must have upset some attendees enough to make them leave. It was too mortifying. She had to get home.

Fatigue kicked in as she walked slowly along the main hallway toward an elevator, noticing a few stragglers in the Court and some chatter and music from the sculpture hall. It definitely felt diminished. Suddenly Jeremy flew out of the nineteenth-century gallery. Damn! He was the last person she wanted to see, but there was no escape. He swerved in front of her, looking like he was about to explode. Rachel tensed.

"How incompetent are you? Do you know what a mess you've caused?" he snapped, one hand on his hip, the other running through his hair. Rachel's face flushed again. "The naturists were supposed to stay away from the kids and the gala. You let them run all over the stairs! They upset the kids and I had to help Naomi get them out of there!"

Even though there seemed to be nobody around, Rachel edged away before she replied. That gave her a moment to gather her thoughts.

"What do you mean, a mess I've caused? Why did Naomi let the kids get on to the mezzanine? And why were they still upstairs so late? It's not my fault they bumped into my group. Naomi caused the mess."

Jeremy shot her a disgusted look. "I gave you one simple instruction and you ignored it. I thought I could trust you to handle this tour. George is furious. Who knows what that means for m—" he caught himself, barely "—for the department?" Damn his ego. *I bet Stinger's been chewed out by George and he's taking it out on me,* she thought. Her throat suddenly felt parched, but she rallied with, "Why did Naomi still have them up here after eight?"

Jeremy ignored her question. "I'm really disappointed in you, Rachel. I expected basic competence. Here I am, working my butt off to get more support for the department, and you're trying to make me look like a fool."

Rachel stared at him, time stopping for a moment as she reviewed the crazy day. Her hangover, Jeremy's command to do this unexpected tour, Naomi's incomprehensible behaviour, her own persistence in spite of the mishaps. She only did the bloody tour to stop him piling up more criticisms against her. She was sick of him making every issue about him. Jerk!

"Make you look like a fool? I think you're capable of doing that yourself. If you'd paid any attention to the realities of the department, you wouldn't have booked a kids' program and a naturist tour on the same night. But you're so focused on your damn visitor engagement centre. You don't have a clue how to run the department day to day, and you let Naomi, the world's most incompetent flake, walk all over you." She paused for a moment, half expecting him to cut her off, but Jeremy just stared at her, mouth agape. "You owe me an apology, Jeremy Stinger." She ignored his puzzled frown. "You threw this ridiculous tour at me this morning and I rose to the occasion to bail you out. It's not my fault things went wrong, and I'm certainly not taking the blame for your fuck-ups."

"We'll see about that on Monday. You have no right to speak to me like that. I…"

But Rachel strode to the elevator, deaf to Stinger's harangue. She felt relieved that she could finally get to her office, but haunted by his expression — a mix of humiliation and exasperation. She might have saved Miss Littlewood, but who was going to save her?

CHAPTER 19
ARTHUR

Arthur gently ushered the Ramsays toward the sculpture hall, feeling like a teacher coaxing a group of unwilling teens. Their grim faces and muttered comments did not bode well for a pleasant drink. He could hardly blame them. He fetched a fortifying whiskey at the bar and joined them as they glumly contemplated the model of the new wing. He raised his glass with a tentative smile, which fell as Barbara snapped, "Your director's an ass. How do you put up with him?"

Because I need a job, thought Arthur. "Barbara, please, forget what he said. It doesn't mean anything. He doesn't know anything about art." Arthur paused, surprised at his own words. He'd just said something that he'd long believed about George, but had disregarded, as long as the director left him alone to do his work. Angry that George had dropped his façade enough to spout such an opinion about his exhibition, he now felt more concerned about appeasing Barbara and her family.

"Really? Is that a qualification for a museum director?" Barbara tossed back the last of her martini.

"It would explain his judgement about our collection," said Alastair, swirling his brandy glass.

Margaret, who had chosen coffee, placed her cup on its saucer and looked at Arthur with concern. "Really, Art, it's very upsetting. He postponed our show from last year, but we still came here tonight, willing to help the campaign. Then he insulted us!"

"He never meant for you to hear that," sputtered Arthur. "It was said in the heat of the moment."

"Why was he ranting in that gallery anyway?" asked Alex. "If he was a real pro, he should have been trying to save the gala. Although it was probably beyond saving at that point."

As if to emphasize Alex's dismissive comment, the jazz trio in the corner started playing "Who's Sorry Now?" The melody was lost on Arthur, who looked from one of the Ramsays to the other in bewilderment, wondering what he could possibly say to appease them.

"You know, Art, he insulted you just as much as he did our collection," Barbara said, her tone reassuringly sympathetic. It didn't last. "But really, tonight was too much. First the schemozzle with the kids and the dancers, then that comment! This place is crazy! Why would I contribute to this damn expansion?" Barbara's voice rose, which caught Victor's attention across the nearly empty room. *Good grief,* Arthur thought, falling back on his favourite expression of distress as he saw the chairman frown. Don't come over. It will make things worse.

"Look, there's tremendous interest in your collection," said Arthur, rousing himself to a more appealing topic. "I know the National Gallery is miffed that they didn't get first dibs on it." He didn't usually indulge in such institutional one-upmanship, but he was desperate. "I can't wait to see the works again on Tuesday." Just four days until the works would arrive and the show's installation would start.

"Hmmm. I know that I made you jump through hoops to get my paintings, but I'm not so sure about lending them now," said Barbara. She looked at the far end of the room, where George had just slunk in. "It would really teach that George Caldwell a lesson if we all cancelled the delivery." Everyone looked at her in shock.

"Barbara, you can't do that," stammered Arthur. It was a night for stammering or sputtering. "You've signed a contract. The works must arrive on Tuesday." He paused, realizing that the gallery's procedures and schedules probably wouldn't have much effect on Barbara, who looked at him defiantly. He plumped for family ties. "Your parents want you to care about this exhibition as much as they do, Barbara, and I hoped tonight would make that happen."

Barbara was about to reply when Alex spoke.

"You know, Barbara's got a point. Maybe that director needs a lesson on the consequences of his bloopers. I don't care how rattled he was by the chaos tonight; he shouldn't let it get the better of him."

Barbara smiled at the unexpected support from her critical brother while Arthur was dumbstruck. Had his old friend gone crazy? What did he mean? Before he could protest, Barbara cried, "I think we should cancel the pick-ups. Let's go somewhere else and talk it over. The night's still young."

"No offence, Art, but this place has put me off." Alastair slammed his empty glass on a table and took his wife's arm. They headed out. Barbara began to follow them, but stopped when Arthur stepped in front of her.

"I ... I ... I don't know what to say," he said forlornly. "This is terrible." Barbara looked at him with a mix of warmth and skepticism.

"It's not your fault, Art. You were a trooper. I'm glad we spent some time together tonight." Her smile widened and Arthur's heart soared. "But that director of yours is unbelievable. Mom and Dad are very upset. I have to help them. I'll see you."

She glided out. Arthur watched her leave, wondering if they really meant to cancel the pick-ups of their works. To his chagrin, it seemed that Barbara's involvement in his exhibition had brought her closer to him, as he'd hoped, and also to her family, but now they were in solidarity against him. He knocked back his whiskey and trudged toward Littlewood Court, too demoralized to look around the sculpture hall for anyone to talk to. The few remaining guests were already corralled by his colleagues and he had no energy for talking up the delights of the new wing now. Then he saw Susannah O'Brien and her party get up from their table. Good grief! He hadn't spoken to her yet, so he dashed across the stage, down the few steps, and swerved through the empty tables to where Mrs. O'Brien stood watching him.

"How nice to see you, Arthur," she said in her haughtiest tone, one hand defensively covering the dark stain on her chest. Her daughter and son-in-law looked at Arthur as if he had crab salad, chicken, and tiramisu trailing down the front of his tuxedo.

"Susannah, hello. I'm sorry I haven't spoken to you already. It's been, ah, an unusual evening…"

"We noticed," said the daughter. "My mother should not have to endure such shenanigans."

"Are you all right? I noticed you were a little indisposed earlier," said Arthur, keeping his eyes on Mrs. O'Brien. Her daughter could be a pain, and Susannah treated him like a favourite nephew who needed her imperious guidance, but Arthur proudly considered her a friend. However, her frosty reply indicated he might be downgraded to unwanted-cousin level.

"Such indignities! First, my dress is ruined. Why were there children up there? Then I saw that naked man prancing around dear Great-Aunt Susannah's bust! I was afraid it was going to topple down the stairs. I've never fainted before in my life! Thank goodness some woman saved it! What is this gallery coming to?"

Arthur was mystified as to why the sculpture almost fell and knew he'd have to look into that. He summoned his most soothing tone. "I'm so sorry. It must have been a great shock for you. There have been a few, ah, surprises tonight." In Arthur's field, work events did not usually involve mollifying outraged patrons, so he had a limited repertoire of phrases at hand.

"Tell your director to keep that man away from there in the future. We don't ask for much in the way of an acknowledgement, but I do like seeing that bronze on the landing. My daughter's even more upset than I am. She thinks I should stop my contribution to the fund and not give anything to the campaign."

"Oh dear," said Arthur. He didn't care if George had to work harder for the campaign, but he did not want his department's budget to suffer because of the gala mishaps. "This is serious. I'm so sorry. You know how I value your support. And George does too. Would it help if he called you?"

"No, I don't care much for that man, as you know. He's too smooth for me. He doesn't really care about Great-Aunt Susannah's collection. You tell him he needs to improve his management style. He's letting our gallery run amok."

"I'm truly sorry," repeated Arthur. It was as likely for him to give George management advice as it was for the director to accept it, but he felt reassured by Susannah's use of the phrase "our gallery." She hadn't abandoned him yet.

"Mother, we should get you home." Mrs. O'Brien's companions moved protectively around her.

"Thank you for stopping by, Arthur. It's the least I should expect. But I'll have to think things over. I'm going to give Margaret Ramsay a call. You know we're old friends."

"Good night," Arthur said with forced smile, apprehensive that a chat with Margaret would only reinforce Susannah's disillusionment with the gallery. He turned and walked into the colonnade, sidestepping around the pianist, who stood wolfing down a plate of Grand Marnier souffle. Arthur sighed. Suddenly he saw his long-anticipated exhibition as a room full of empty frames, their bare interiors mocking his efforts.

CHAPTER 20
AMANDA

"Incredible event, Amanda," said Zach. "The dance really made it. My idea, you know. Too bad people weren't watching it much." He downed his Scotch, took his girlfriend's arm, and left the sculpture hall.

Amanda twirled her martini glass, uninterested in drinking its contents. Half of her table had left after the dessert, and she wished Zach Drake had joined them. She had struggled to make small talk with him and his companion in the echoing sculpture hall, so recently alive with gleeful chatter and anticipation. She didn't care that Zach seemed offended by the fact that so much chaos had happened during the dance. Where the hell had those kids come from? And naturists on the landing! From her table, she had caught George's activity: dashing after departing patrons, a short unfriendly-looking chat with Simon, leading a furious Victor into the sculpture hall. While trying to detain her departing tablemates, whose snarky remarks implied their lowered support for the campaign, she thought that George must be apoplectic that his big night had fallen apart. She felt smug about that, but also concerned that problems with the campaign could affect her. Nine ten. She didn't care if she was supposed to stay until ten thirty. What was the point? Anyone she wanted to talk to had fled.

By the time Amanda reached the cloakroom, there was still a line-up of departing guests. She stood for a moment, wondering what she would see outside. Were Justin and his collective there? She noticed that the guards at the desk appeared agitated as they cast wary glances her way.

Outside, there appeared to be more people here than inside the gallery. It took a moment for Amanda to sort out what was happening. On her left, several disgruntled-looking gala attendees stood watching. A few steps down, on the sidewalk, five men and women, dressed mainly in black, slowly walked in a circle, handing out leaflets to the departing guests who threaded their way through them. A few carried signs saying Support Canadian Artists Now. Justin waved and ran toward her, his jacket flying open to reveal his T-shirt bearing the same slogan.

"How come they're leaving so soon?" he asked, handing her a leaflet. "Although it's good for us. We thought we'd have to be here for hours."

"There have been some unscheduled events," said Amanda, glancing at the leaflet. She had time to read the first two lines, "Support Canadian Artists Now: Why does the Toronto Art Gallery need to hire an American artist to produce a sculpture for its new wing?" But she stopped when Justin asked, "You mean like the cameras staying on?"

She looked at him with a frown. What was he talking about? He raised his eyebrows and nodded toward the window where the projections from the various *Gestes* cameras appeared. A group of people stood there, transfixed, then drooped with a collective sigh and turned away.

"They must be off now," said Justin. "How did they get left on? People have been watching stuff the whole time we've been here."

"Good question. I've no idea why they were on."

"Some people who left about half an hour ago were upset when they saw it. They weren't dressed up. One of them gave an interview to the TV crew. He seemed pretty cool, but others were grumbling about being nude on camera."

At that moment, a man wielding a camera on his shoulder left the projection area and descended to the sidewalk where the protesters circled.

"We didn't expect media here, but it's good for our cause. I'd better speak to them. Bye." Justin ran down the steps.

"Bye." Amanda watched him give a leaflet to a woman who appeared to be with the cameraman and begin talking animatedly. She strolled over to the window where the projection had just ended and stared at the dark space. The ramifications of the cameras being left on after five were dawning on her. Embarrassment for the gallery, if any of the rotations showed those damn kids or naturists. The nineteenth-century gallery! When she had ducked in there with Steven, she had never thought of its camera because it was supposed to be turned off. Shit! This night was too much! Justin's protest was the only part that could possibly work out well for her. She hoped that some of the departing guests would care enough to raise a stink about an important commission going to an American artist.

"Amanda, do you have a comment?" She turned to her right to see Simon Kinsella brandishing one of Justin's leaflets. He read from it:

> Director George Caldwell has announced that American sculptor Daniel Reid will get this prestigious commission. We believe that the people of Toronto want to see local, regional, and national Canadian artists in their art gallery. Use your influence as patriotic members. Tell the director and the board they are making a big mistake! Insist that they need to change this decision now.

"Strong stuff," he said. "This collective must have an inside line. The director only announced this commission tonight and they already have leaflets protesting it. Care to comment?"

"I always support artists standing up for their rights," said Amanda, falling back on something she'd said once in an interview. How annoying that this reporter, of all people, popped up now.

"Do you support the collective's demand that the director withdraw the commission?" Simon persisted.

"I couldn't possibly comment." She looked around wildly. Thank god, a taxi was slowing down.

"That's okay. I thought I was only going to write a dance review, but tonight's provided a lot more to investigate."

"That's my taxi! Good night." Amanda darted through a few departing attendees and the protesters as Simon scribbled in his notebook.

CHAPTER 21
RACHEL

"Excuse me!" Rachel said to no avail as Amanda brushed her aside to grab the taxi she had waved at. As Rachel looked for another, she also took in the activity outside the gallery. Departing gala attendees were backed up waiting for the valet parking attendants to bring their cars. Impatient and muttering, they looked disdainfully at the group of artists around Justin, who was energetically speaking to a reporter. The reporter who had been with TAG Camp! Justin's group must be the protesters that the guard had mentioned.

A taxi slowed down and Rachel grabbed it without fending off any competitors. She felt too tired to worry about the implications of all that action as she rode home to Durie Street, glad to have a quick escape after the stressful blow-up with Jeremy. Her husband, Nick, was still out rehearsing with his band, The Briefs, so she got ready for bed, feeling tired yet eager to tell him all about the calamitous evening. She woke from a light doze when he entered their bedroom around quarter to eleven.

"How did it go?" he asked after pecking her cheek. He sat on the edge of the bed and sipped from his bottle of beer. His lopsided smile and mischievous brown eyes told her that she had not heard the last joke about her unusual tour. "Give me the naked truth."

"Oh, shut up. I've heard enough puns for one night," she said, slapping his arm. Then, staring up at the ceiling, she added, "You won't believe this. I chewed out Jeremy."

"Stinger?" asked Nick, looking at her in surprise. He knew Rachel's private names for her colleagues better than their real ones. "So you won't be asking him for a reference?"

Rachel frowned for a moment, then remembered yesterday's job interview. Only yesterday? It seemed ages ago.

"No," she said with a brief laugh. "Good thing I found other people for that. I think Stinger lost a bit of his golden glow tonight."

"Did he upset the nudists?"

"No, actually he was never near them. But they did get upset." Rachel told Nick the whole tale.

"You actually saved Miss Littlewood's bust? That alone should get you the promotion. I bet Stinger's never done anything that noble."

"Yeah, and I've got the bruises to prove it," said Rachel, holding out her right arm. The weight of the bronze had left a purplish-green mark. "The guards think I deserve an award."

"Wow. Shouldn't that thing have been bolted down? Can you sue them?"

"You tell me, you're the lawyer. I have a feeling I'm in enough trouble without bringing legal action against the gallery."

"But you told off Stinger?"

"Yeah, it just came out. Shit, I think I even called him Stinger!"

By this time, it was eleven o'clock and Nick turned on the television to watch the late-night local news. When the anchor mentioned the Toronto Art Gallery, Rachel tensed up. She recognized the handsome, athletic-looking man in a suede jacket standing in front of TAG's front façade.

"Oh no, it's that maniac Damian."

"That's the guy you were grabbing? You didn't say how cool he is. Even with his clothes on."

Rachel slapped Nick's arm again. "I was not grabbing him. I was rescuing Miss Littlewood. Let me listen."

"We prefer the term naturists. It's more sympatico than nudist. Shows the connection with nature. It's a connection we all have. Being naked feels good." An identification bar at the bottom of the screen stated: Damian Nowak, Yoga Instructor, Corporate Consultant, and Naturist.

"How did your experience of looking at art change by being allowed to do the tour au naturel?" The camera switched briefly to a female reporter, the same one Rachel had seen at the gallery.

"It was fantastic. We love it when we can do the normal things we enjoy, whether that's yoga, or looking at art, in the way that we prefer. It wasn't quite as exclusive as we expected, but my group and I are thrilled that the gallery was open to this."

An angry-looking bearded man thrust his head over Damian's shoulder. "Damn right it wasn't exclusive! This gallery has no respect for naturists!" The reporter directed her microphone toward the man, but Damian smoothly shouldered him away.

She refocused on Damian. "Do you think you'll return to TAG?"

"I do corporate consulting too. I'm sure TAG could use my expertise. And yes, I think some of my group would like to do this again."

After thanking him, the reporter turned to the camera and said, "I'll bet it was a revealing experience!"

Rachel groaned. "You know, I saw the reporter and cameraman still hanging around when I left. They must have filmed him earlier."

The reporter continued. "That wasn't the only new event at the Toronto Art Gallery tonight. We also looked at a program for children called TAG Camp."

The segment showed a few seconds of the children building their sculptures and a few seconds of Jeremy saying the gallery strove to reach different audiences in innovative ways.

"Smooth," said Nick, while Rachel rolled her eyes. Then she gasped.

"Passersby can get a sense of the fascinating activity going on inside the Toronto Art Gallery through the current contemporary show *Gestes*," said the reporter.

"What's that?" asked Nick, frowning at the television. "It's you, hon!"

Rachel's eyes widened in horror. A short clip showed the brightly lit landing of the grand staircase, with her tackling the bust, Damian swaying, and a few naturists descending from the left. The cameraman had filmed the projection! To her relief, it quickly switched to the empty *Gestes* gallery.

"Oh my god! Of all the nights for the cameras to remain on! I hope nobody recognizes me."

"Looks like you were fleshing out the situation," Nick said, dodging Rachel's playful punch. "Heroically, of course."

"Stinger won't see it that way. He'll use it against me. I wish he'd just disappear."

"I have clients who could help with that." Nick grinned. "Let me know if you need a lawyer."

An image flashed across Rachel's fatigued mind: Jeremy catapulting head over heels down a long staircase. That was too much, even for Stinger. The reporter continued, "The gallery also attracted some protesters tonight."

Rachel leaned forward. She recognized Justin at the microphone, saying something about supporting Canadian artists. So that's why he'd been there. Suddenly she felt fed up with TAG's chaos and wanted only to catch up on her much-needed sleep before she faced the fallout.

"Monday's going to be hell."

"Well," said Nick, "there's only one thing left to say about all that."

"What?"

He raised his beer bottle. "Bottoms up."

SATURDAY

CHAPTER 22
GEORGE

"Ready, aim, fire!" George woke up with a start. With the relief that follows a bad dream, he realized that he was in his own bed, not in front of a firing squad. Since becoming director, he'd often felt like he faced one, trembling before the ire of board members, donors, patrons, members, staff, the media, and the public, ready to tumble like the balsa wood walls of his cherished architectural model. Except that he had accomplished that demolition himself. And more than that last night.

A shower did little to lift George's mood. Alone in the kitchen, as his wife had taken his sons to their swimming lessons, he swallowed two Tylenols to soothe his pounding head and twinging knee and poured a mug of coffee. Saturday morning's *Tribune* lay on the table, open to an article by Simon Kinsella. He braced himself to read it.

TAG Laid Bare

Simon Kinsella

Arts Reporter

Yesterday evening, an unusual constellation of events glittered at our illustrious Toronto Art Gallery. As reported in this newspaper, the TAG21 Campaign launched with a gala reception and dinner, intended to lure pledges to the $150 million expansion project. Three other apparently unscheduled events also took place: a naturist tour requested by a wealthy donor; TAG Camp, a new sleepover program piloted by the Education and Public Programs department; and a protest by a group of artists outside the gallery.

The naturists attended courtesy of Barbara Ramsay, whose family has a major collection of Canadian art, *Terrain and Town: The Ramsay Canadian Collection*, that will open at TAG next month. Ms. Ramsay, an occasional figure on Toronto's social scene, requested this private tour for her naturist yoga group as a condition for lending her own works to her family's show. While she didn't require that gallery staff join the disrobing, despite the undoubted artistic legacy of the nude figure, it does seem like moneyed donors are free to indulge any personal whim. In spite of the staff's best efforts to keep the two groups apart from each other, and from the gala, they all collided.

The TAG Camp children made an unscheduled appearance on the mezzanine overlooking Littlewood Court, surprising not only the well-heeled diners below, but some of the wait staff, who lost their aim in pouring wine and serving salads. One recipient of such misplaced dishing-up was unfortunately Mrs. Susannah O'Brien, great-niece of the gallery's founder, Susannah Littlewood, and stalwart supporter, often asked for donations to the arts.

The gala's planned entertainment featured the Avalon Dance Company, who premiered their new composition, *Generosity*. The children seized this moment to return to the gala by chasing the dancers down the grand staircase. This disturbance did not faze the resolute performers, who carried on with their stirring tribute to philanthropy. But the gala attendees were distracted again when one of the naturists decided to hold a yoga pose on the landing of the staircase.

It was too much for Mrs. O'Brien, who fainted. Contacted for a comment, she said, "In all my years of attending gallery events, I've never experienced anything like it. I think a dance performance was a lovely addition to a gala, but a nude man wrapping himself around the bust of my great-aunt was too much! He almost threw it down the stairs! I've never fainted before in my life. I don't know what the gallery's coming to. The board will hear from me." TAG's donor relations staff may need more than smelling salts to revive her benevolence.

Five members of the Parkdale Artists Collective chose last night to protest outside the gallery about TAG's announcement at the gala: to commission American artist Daniel Reid to create a statement sculpture for the new wing. According to organizer Justin Lord, "The Toronto Art Gallery should award such a prestigious commission to a Canadian artist. We urge the gala guests, TAG members, and the public to contact the gallery and demand that it reverse this terrible decision."

Passersby had a choice of listening to the artists' chants or watching the constant stream of images from different rooms inside TAG. Part of the brilliant *Gestes* exhibition by Quebec artist Simone Brodeur, the exterior projection, in a prominent place on the façade, documents the comings and goings of staff and visitors inside. Normally turned off when the gallery closes for the night, by an extraordinary masterstroke of coordination, the cameras were left on. Observers caught the costume-clad TAG Camp kids in a sculpture gallery and then the naturists in the *Gestes* gallery and on the landing. Presumably such exposure was not a scheduled part of their tour. One witty observer asked, "Are birthday suits the new dress code here?"

Another camera caught the director, George Caldwell, holding an impromptu meeting in the 19th-century gallery, one that seemed to upset the participants. No doubt he, and the chair of the board of trustees, Victor Drake, are pondering the gala's outcome today. Neither man could be reached for comment, but, in keeping with TAG's new desire to uncover the naked truth, we assume that they will soon reveal all.

"Fuck!" spat George, sloshing coffee as he slammed down his mug. As if the TV coverage, caught when he returned home unexpectedly early from the truncated gala, wasn't bad enough, that damn Kinsella had weaseled his way in somehow. Who the hell let in the little prick? He noticed that a short review of the dance company's performance, also by Kinsella, ran beside the larger article. Hmph. That must explain why he was there. Fuck! Of all the nights for that bastard to be at TAG. He'd caught that damn artists' protest too.

The phone rang. George's sinking feeling that the caller would be Victor proved to be correct. He, too, had read the *Tribune*.

"Where does the little shit get his dirt? I'd like to deal with that scumbag! Why don't you fire whoever it is?"

Spoken like someone who runs a non-unionized workplace. "He wasn't spying, Victor. He was there. He's just a hack. Don't worry about it," George said weakly, vowing to make staff pay for the embarrassment that Kinsella dredged up. He cradled his throbbing head and waited for Victor's next blast.

"Damn it, George, I don't need any more calls from friends asking me what kind of gallery this is. I have better things to do than try to explain why a bunch of nudists showed up at an exclusive dinner. And why kids were running around. Can't the little brats just come with their schools? What next? A daycare?"

At this point, George felt so hostile toward the education department that he wouldn't put it past them to be planning just such a program, as another inclusive initiative. However, he couldn't worry about that now. He had to appease Victor and, he suspected, many others who would be calling him soon.

"Victor, can we meet next week? I'm sure we can call some people and convince them that the gallery is still worth supporting."

"Supporting! We were supposed to be rolling in pledges and instead we're a laughingstock. This raises serious questions about your leadership. I'll be talking to other board members."

"What do you mean?" asked George, chilled. He knew all too well what it meant. Some members would be salivating at the opportunity to wrap Friday's fiasco around his neck and hang him with it.

"Someone has to pay for this schemozzle, George."

"And I'll make sure they do. Come on, Victor. We've been such a great team so far. I'm sure we can get the campaign back on track. When can you come in?" George asked, trying to deflect Victor's outrage.

"I'll let you know on Monday. About that other thing."

George tensed. Here it comes. Victor never abandoned his concern over the donation of his collection for long. George resented the control that the chairman was trying to exert. His agreement to help Victor obtain the highest possible tax credit had seemed easy and worth doing in order to secure the ten-million-dollar contribution to the building campaign. But once George knew that such a large donation required a second appraisal, he had an uneasy feeling about Victor's repeated urging that Lionel Hathaway, and only Hathaway, be the one to do it.

"I want you to use Hathaway for the second appraisal. You've got the letter from him."

"It's unusual for a donor to suggest appraisers. That's the job of the curator handling the donation."

"What is this? My collection isn't fake!"

"We're not talking about authenticity, Victor. We don't need an authenticator. We just need two honest appraisers who can assess the market for British horse paintings and produce similar evaluations."

"And that's what Hathaway can do. Christ, I'm helping you, George. From the way you run your gallery, you could bloody do with some help."

George noted that the chairman had not picked up on his use of the word "honest." Victor's obsession had sunk on his own priority list at the moment, given the necessity to salvage the campaign and possibly his job. He strove to keep the appraisal on the back burner.

"Victor, our priority right now is the campaign. Let's talk on Monday."

Reluctantly Victor agreed. George put the receiver down. The phone rang again and continued to do so throughout the weekend.

CHAPTER 23
ARTHUR

Arthur tossed aside the *Tribune* and stared morosely at the book-lined wall of his living room. He had no idea how Kinsella had found the scoop on the gala's mishaps, but that concerned him less than the comments from Susannah O'Brien. Trust Kinsella to catch her in a rare moment of outrage. He wasn't sure how much influence she had with the board of trustees, but he knew that they would not want to see the founder's great-niece so distressed. He would have to make amends with her, but right now he was more obsessed with the Ramsays. Thank goodness that Kinsella had not run into them last night. A late-night call to Alex had confirmed their decision to cancel the pick-up of their works on Monday. Although Arthur had desperately tried to persuade him to reconsider then and again this morning, he was adamant. Alex and his parents were on their way back to Kingston now.

This was a disaster. He had arranged the pick-up date with the exhibitions head months ago. She had scheduled two members of the installations staff to accompany the art shippers, an outside company, to Kingston, to ensure all the packing could happen in two days, bringing those works, and Barbara's, safely to the gallery a month ahead of the opening. With the paintings on hand, she and her team could focus on all the other aspects of an exhibition, and the inevitable time-consuming glitches, without worrying about the most important element.

He felt betrayed that his sensible friend had taken up his mercurial sister's threat.

Barbara was willful, but also carefree. He'd never seen her so indignant before, but then he really hadn't seen much of her in the past two decades, in contrast to how much he'd seen of her last night. They had been getting on so well at the dinner, before the gala fell apart. Arthur had no idea of her feelings for him, yet hoped to appeal to her to save his exhibition.

He could not face calling the exhibitions head right away. Instead he dialled Barbara's number. No answer. He kept trying in between getting dressed and doing a few errands. After swallowing his pride about admitting the exhibition was off track, he called the exhibitions head to tell her about the cancelled pick-up. Around three o'clock, frustrated by Barbara's non-answering, he decided to walk to her condo. The fresh air would do him good.

Along the way from his flat on Palmerston to her condo on Walmer Road, he stopped at a florist's to buy two bouquets of flowers, thinking that he would go to Susannah O'Brien's Rosedale home after seeing Barbara. While feeling that George was the bigger culprit in sparking the Ramsays' ire, Arthur knew it was his job to appease his patron.

To his dismay, he saw Damian standing in front of the residents' listing in the foyer of Barbara's building. Good grief.

"Oh, hello," mumbled Arthur.

"Hi, Arthur," said Damian, breaking into a wide smile. "Great tour. Thanks again. That was a lot of fun. And I got to speak to that TV reporter afterward. Did you see me? I've had so many calls. Naturist yoga is really gonna take off."

"Wonderful," said Arthur through clenched teeth as he speculated why Damian was there. He didn't want to confront Barbara with him hanging around. Or doing yoga.

"Are you here to see Barbara? She's still pissed off at the gallery. You guys should shape up. I run corporate development workshops, you know. My coaching has a track record of improving communication and team-building. Maybe the gallery should book me."

"Um, not my territory, I'm afraid," said Arthur, picturing gallery staff sitting naked in Littlewood Court, meditating. He had no idea if that what was what went on in corporate development, but suspected that human resources would show little interest in Damian's approach, whatever it was. "But, yes, I'm here to see Barbara. If you'll excuse me."

"Hope you have better luck than I did. She must be pissed off at me too," said Damian. "I might be calling the gallery to see about holding a yoga class there. Cool spaces. Bye."

"Great," muttered Arthur as he turned to find Barbara's code. A moment later he rode the elevator up to her floor, relieved that she had let him in.

Even with no make-up and casually dressed in a loose white tunic and black leggings, Barbara looked fantastic, and to his relief accepted one of the bouquets graciously.

"I just saw Damian outside," he said, following her into the kitchen.

"Oh, really?" She sounded indifferent as she arranged the flowers in a vase.

Arthur wasn't sure how to respond to Barbara's cool tone, then remembered Damian's bragging. "He said something about being on TV. When was that?"

"Apparently there was a cameraman and reporter on hand. Was that for the kids? They hung around outside until Damian and the group left the gallery. They interviewed him about the pleasures of looking at art as naturists. I didn't see it but several members of my group caught him on the late-night news and called me about it. Apparently he's a media natural. Never met a camera he doesn't like."

"Hmmm," said Arthur, alarmed by the thought of more naturist tours. "Barbara, I need to speak to you about last night. You haven't returned my calls."

"Would you like some tea?" Barbara poured two cups, then led him from the kitchen to the dining room, where the four paintings from her parents' collection hung on sea-green walls. Arthur had admired the colour on his one visit two years ago, when he had accompanied the photographer who documented the works for the catalogue. How far away that seemed now, an idyllic moment in his exhibition's progress before it collapsed in last night's tempest. Two paintings faced him, one a loosely-painted scene of a woman reading under a shady tree, the other an equally impressionistic depiction of a couple on a sunny cliff. Seated under them, Barbara looked at him with a half-smile, almost as if she wanted to taunt him with their nearness, the desired objects now out of his reach.

"This is serious, Barbara. We can't cancel an exhibition a month before it's due to open."

Barbara twirled a strand of her red-gold hair in her right hand and gazed at him over her teacup.

"Why not?" she asked. "George did it. A year ago, when he wanted to make way for his boring Monet show. He doesn't like our dingy old paintings anyway."

"I think we can all agree — even George — that *Monet's Moments* was a mistake. One the gallery has already paid for," said Arthur gravely, his hands clasped in front of him.

But Barbara wasn't finished. "It's not just that. The naturist tour, my one, tiny condition, was a disaster. I asked for an exclusive event and what do I get? A bunch of kids running around! And those calls from members of my group: they're angry that a cameraman popped up. People outside the gallery saw it on some screen. Really, Art, that's a breach of the privacy we were promised. A naturist tour should be treated with respect. What kind of place do you work in?"

"The cameraman deleted whatever he filmed of your group," said Arthur. He'd heard that from the guards on his way out last night. "What the people saw outside was something else," he continued, in exasperation. He had his own qualms about the gallery's management but resented her questioning it. "To be truthful, those cameras should not have been left on. Those projections don't last long and few people would have seen it. I don't know how it happened, Barbara, and I'm very sorry ... Damian didn't seem bothered by it."

"Damian would cheerfully give an interview in the nude," Barbara retorted. She looked away for a moment, then met his gaze once again, this time with a kindlier look in her eyes. "Thanks for telling me that the TV crew were dealt with. That's reassuring, although I don't know what my group will do about that other thing — a projection? But I'm still angry about the insult to my family's collection. Your director's a jerk."

Arthur suppressed his desire to agree with her.

"It wasn't his finest moment," he said. "He was stressed about the disastrous gala. He was worried that people were going to be so upset by the disturbances during dinner that they'd decline to contribute. He said it in the heat of the moment. I'll make sure he apologizes."

"He'd better," she said, tossing her hair. Then she smiled. "It's been a nice change to have Alex on my side for once, instead of reprimanding me for being irresponsible, as usual. I think I'm being very responsible, standing up for Mom and Dad. They don't deserve to be treated like that."

Good grief, thought Arthur, sipping his tea. Naturally placid, he didn't have a huge repertoire of expressions of distress. Sibling rivalry turned into sibling solidarity? Against him! But he'd seen another side of Barbara last night, when she had confided in him about her daughter.

"But Barbara, really, to cancel at the last minute. That's treatment I've never had from a lender." He squared his shoulders as Barbara looked at him in surprise. "I'm sorry that you were offended, but quite frankly, you're overreacting. And you're ignoring a signed contract to lend your works. It may not mean anything to you, but you're destroying my professional reputation. And if you're so concerned about getting closer to Lily, I don't see how this is going to help." He took a deep breath as her eyes widened. "I'm begging you to reconsider and lend your works for the exhibition."

"What's Lily got to do with it?" she asked, her face crumpling a little.

"You told me about her last night. You want a better relationship. How are you going to handle her teenage moods if you blow up at every unfortunate gaffe?" Arthur was surprised at himself.

Counselling was not his strong point, but his patience with Barbara's moods was wearing out.

"You sound just like my ex-husband," she said with a pout.

"Well, I might have been a bit forward, but come on, Barbara. You demanded a tour for your naturist group as a condition of lending your paintings and now you've reneged on that very promise. Just because my damn director blew his mouth off again."

Barbara looked startled. "That's not like you, Art."

"No, it isn't," said Arthur, getting up. "Forget I said that. I'm upset. This is the worst day of my professional career. We've got to get on with this exhibition. Please call your parents and talk it over. I promise that I'll speak to George on Monday and he'll apologize. You know where to reach me. Goodbye."

Arthur turned and headed for the door, too agitated to trust himself to say more. He felt her stunned gaze follow him — he would be willing to bet she wasn't used to men walking out on her. He put his hand on the doorknob, then remembered the other bouquet of flowers. When he turned back, he saw Barbara holding it as she stood in the doorway to her kitchen.

"Art…"

"Um, yes, thank you. I need those," he said, reaching out for the flowers. "Unfortunately, you're not the only upset woman I have to see today."

"Art, maybe I've been hasty. I don't know. Can we talk about it over dinner?"

Arthur looked at her in surprise. She was serious. He readily agreed to meet her at a restaurant at eight.

"You won't wear that jacket, will you?" Barbara asked with a slight smile. He looked down at his well-worn twill jacket. What was wrong with it? But if he could agree to lead a tour for naturists for the sake of his exhibition, he supposed he could upgrade his wardrobe.

"I can find something less rumpled," he said, returning her smile. Feeling more buoyant than when he'd arrived, he headed for the subway, hoping his next visit would end as amicably, if not with the same romantic potential.

MONDAY

CHAPTER 24
ARTHUR

Arthur had barely hung up his coat on Monday morning when he was summoned to the director's office. He braced himself for the expected confrontation, fortified by Barbara's softening attitude. George wasted no time launching a new attack.

"Arthur! I hope you've come to apologize for the mess you caused with those naturists. I've had to listen to board members complaining about the gala. Some of them are friends of Susannah O'Brien's and can't believe that we'd insult the founder and her family like that. And now Susannah's giving interviews to that bloody Kinsella about how disappointed she is with us. What are you going to do about it? You know I leave the care and coddling of Susannah O'Brien to you. Do I have to handle that now too?"

Arthur paused. Normally he found George's anger intimidating and his impulse was to appease him and escape as soon as possible. But the phrase "dingy old paintings" reverberated in his mind again, as it had throughout the weekend. He had hit a wall. He'd had enough of George Caldwell's browbeating and dismissal of his department. Time to stand up for Canadian historical art. "Well, if you handle her as well as you did the Ramsays, I think we'd be even worse off than we are now."

"What? How dare you talk to me like that?" George shot up from his chair and braced his fists on his desk as he loomed across it. "Don't you know I'm trying to save the campaign, which you did your best to sabotage?"

"George, the Ramsays were so angry on Friday that they cancelled today's pick-up of their collection."

"What the fuck! How did you let that happen?" George's face began to redden.

"I did everything humanly possible to keep that exhibition on track. I even managed to do so while facilitating an unusual donor request. We could have fulfilled that a year ago if you hadn't bumped their exhibition for that *Monet's Moments* ... show. But I appeased them and everything was fine until you expressed your opinion of their collection. They don't want to lend their works. There's no point attacking me. You should be asking yourself how *you* let it happen."

George strode around the office. With an impassive expression, Arthur folded his arms and watched him. His satisfaction with his speech gave way to anxiety when George stopped by the smashed model of the gallery. It occurred to Arthur that the director's hot temper might have caused that damage. He tensed, fearing that George might take a swing at him. But the director kept his hands in his pockets as he exhaled in exasperation, met Arthur's eyes for a brief moment, then flopped into his chair.

"Christ. Obviously, I fucked up. Friday night did not go as planned and now I have all this shit to clean up."

"As do I. Which I've been working on. I've convinced Barbara to reconsider and to talk to her parents. If they change their minds, Alex will too. But they need an apology." Arthur had a feeling that "I fucked up" was the best he would get from George about his insult, but he could live with that half-hearted apology if the director summoned a convincing one for the Ramsays. He watched the director swivel in his chair, chin in hand.

"I apologized on Friday. Christ, what do they want?"

"A sincere, convincing apology. It may feel like grovelling, but we can't cancel a show that's been years in the making. TAG's reputation would suffer," said Arthur, slyly appealing to George's ego, certain that the gallery's reputation mattered more to the director than that of a mere curator.

"It already has," muttered George, running his fingers through his hair. "All right. Do I have to call all of them?"

"No, just Alastair and Margaret. If they come around, the others will."

"I'll get to it right away. Christ, how many people do I have to phone? I suppose you think you can handle Susannah O'Brien."

"I already have."

"Good. Keep her away from that Kinsella. The last thing I need is him on my back."

Arthur could relate — the last thing he needed was George on his own back. He spent most of the day trying to sort out what aspects of the Ramsay exhibition could carry on while they waited for the paintings to arrive. Nothing as drastic as this had happened with his previous shows, but he had often had to concoct a Plan B, while keeping as cool as a ship's captain issuing orders from the bridge in rough weather. He ensured that the technicians would finish painting the walls in the temporary exhibition galleries and that the art shipment company could collect some new acquisitions sooner than planned, in lieu of the big job cancelled today. The gallery was one of its major customers, so, although this upended everyone's schedule, they agreed.

CHAPTER 25
GEORGE

George sat staring at the architectural model of the new wing in his office, or rather its ruins. He hadn't yet notified the architect of the damage he'd done last Friday. Was it only three days ago? It felt much longer. All weekend, he had fielded calls from agitated board members, and just now had endured the embarrassing meeting with Arthur. He knew that calling the Ramsays should be job number one, but he had a new problem to deal with first.

John had forwarded him an email with the subject line "Urgent: Read this." The offending message had been posted to the MUSEUM-P listserv, a huge email list for museum and gallery professionals in Canada and the States, which George looked at occasionally. He relied on John and his assistant to monitor the list more consistently, and had no time for it today, until he saw John's warning. George fumed. The email was from Jeremy, written last night, to a friend in another gallery.

Hi Pamela,

It's been a while! You would not believe what's been happening at TAG, or maybe you would, given what I've told you before. On Friday night, we held our big gala fundraiser to launch the building campaign. Our fearless leader, George, and his sidekick, Victor, had high hopes of getting lots of pledges for their new wing. As you know, this was a great opportunity for me to pitch to donors for a visitor engagement centre, which this gallery needs so much. George seems to think attendance will increase just by making more room for old paintings of horses! Ha! People need something to do. We can't expect them to be happy just looking at art, especially if the curators write the labels. Anyway, I was more diplomatic on Friday, using the Singer charm you're always teasing me about, and convinced a few key people of its importance. I know they'll be sending in their pledges soon, and I'll make sure I get credit, even if I have to trample those development bitches to do so.

I think I did a better job getting pledges than our revered director. I heard he actually insulted a lender last Friday! Unbelievable for someone who thinks he's such a great leader. I wish he'd finally get off his butt and post the head job. No serious internal competition. Well, there's Rachel Burns. I've told you about her. She's been at TAG for decades, coordinates adult programs. She's good at details but has no experience with interpretive planning or anything innovative. And she screwed up royally on Friday, ignoring my instructions about a VIP tour group and letting them run amok. They happened to be naturists, and we also had the pilot of my brilliant new kids' program, a sleepover. How those got booked on the same night is beyond me; maybe Rachel had something to do with it. I instructed her to keep the two groups away from each other, but she goofed up. Caused some ruckus. Hardly management material, right? She thinks she's so organized. Well, she'll get a surprise tomorrow morning. I don't know how I'm expected to run an education department with people like her in it.

> I hope your boss has finally smartened up and let you
> run the meetings!
>
> Jeremy

To his relief, George read that the listserv manager had deleted the reply-all email, presumably sent erroneously, with a reminder to subscribers about not posting personal messages. The damn thing was probably up long enough to effect some damage. He seethed as he saw his message button flashing on his phone and his bursting inbox. But he had to deal with Jeremy first. While he waited for him to come up, he reread Kinsella's article. Damn that hack! He'd have to chew out whoever let him in on Friday, even it was just to cover the dance. Damn those cameras! One of his many tasks for the morning was discovering why they were left on.

He kept reading as John and Jeremy entered his office and sat down. George folded the paper, slammed it on his desk, looked at the deputy director and said, "Bugger that Kinsella. It's bad enough that all that shit happened, but I hoped we'd be able to contain it. How the hell did he get in?"

"Good promo for TAG Camp though," said Jeremy. "And the naturist tour makes the gallery look very open."

As George looked at Jeremy for the first time, he noted the younger man's cheery mask shielding an inner trembling. Good. He'd had it with this twerp.

"Do you think so?" asked George slowly, feigning interest in Jeremy's opinion. "I'm so glad to hear your point of view, Mr. Singer. You seem to have adopted a very open approach yourself." He fingered a piece of paper on his desk.

Jeremy swallowed hard. George lifted the sheet of paper and held it by one corner.

"Here's the evidence. You were being quite open in sharing your opinions over the weekend. Opinions about this gallery, my management, your colleagues. And your job prospects." He waved the paper at Jeremy, who looked confused, then aghast as his eyes widened in realization.

John said, "Don't our email protocols spell out the danger of using reply-all?"

"I don't know if danger is the right word, John," said George, rising and coming around to lean on the front of his desk, near Jeremy. "Maybe for the sender, but it's very useful for those of us privileged to read his communications. You've got a way with words, Jeremy." He glanced down at the paper. "Fearless leader. Sidekick. Singer charm. Insult a lender. Get off his butt. Development bitches. Hardly management material." He lowered the paper and loomed over Jeremy. "I gather you think you're management material?"

"I … I … I can explain," stammered Jeremy. He craned his head back to look up, but the director's furious expression startled him and he quickly moved his eyes to his lap.

"Really? Let's hear it."

"I … I … I can't explain. I'm sorry. I didn't mean it," said Jeremy. "I was upset. On your behalf, of course. I know how much the night meant to you. Me too. I made some fantastic contacts with potential sponsors for the visitor engagement—"

"Do you think I give a fuck about your visitor engagement centre?" shouted George, swinging back to his chair and glaring at Jeremy. "We don't even know if there'll be one. I don't even know why you were there. You should have been attending to your staff and their damn programs, making sure they stayed out of the way. Not swanning with donors. That's for senior management, development, and curators." He paused, relishing Jeremy's shocked expression.

"I'm afraid your explanation, such as it is, doesn't help you, Jeremy," said George. "Attacking management and your colleagues in such an unseemly manner is cause for dismissal. You obviously think you deserve better than to work at the Toronto Art Gallery, so I'm happy to help you on your way. You're fired."

"Fired?" gasped Jeremy, his jaw dropping. He looked from George to John in disbelief.

"Yes, fired. What did you expect? That we called you in here to congratulate you on your communication skills? Other museum directors are on that list, you know. God knows what calls I'm going to get, on top of all the other shit on my desk. Were you expecting congratulations on how you run your department? Leave now. John will give you the lowdown."

Jeremy slowly rose from his chair in a state of shock and meekly followed John from the room. George leaned back in his chair, cradling the back of his head in his clasped hands. He allowed himself a moment of satisfaction, as he had wanted some staff to pay for Friday's debacle and Jeremy had set himself up to take the fall. Obnoxious twit! George knew his decision meant another meeting with John to figure out what to do with education, but that could wait. His assistant opened the door to show in the manager of security. After several more meetings, he found some time to call Alastair Ramsay and grovel. His apology was accepted.

When he called Arthur to relay the news that the show was back on track, George was relieved that he only reached his voice mail. That made it easier to revert to his preferred brusque tone. Although he felt secretly ashamed of his unguarded outburst, he couldn't bring himself to eat crow again. Among all the other reminders of the gala's disastrous fallout, Victor's quasi-threat about his job reverberated disturbingly at the back of his mind. He'd have to make sure the chairman did not pursue it. As he contemplated his unenviable situation, his knee twinged again. Damn! He popped two Tylenols and braced himself for his next meeting.

THURSDAY

CHAPTER 26
RACHEL

You know the job. Blow them away. Rachel mentally repeated Nick's words like a mantra as she walked from the streetcar stop to the gallery on Thursday. Why she needed that mantra was due to the gala aftermath. It hit the education and public programs department in several ways, starting on Monday, as the beleaguered receptionist fielded a barrage of telephone calls.

"Four parents want their money back because they say their children are traumatized, one mother commends us for taking such a broad-minded approach to children's education, two other naturist groups want to book their own tours, somebody wants to know when we're offering yoga classes, and two men from that tour say they're going to sue the gallery for invasion of privacy. Who's going to handle these?" she wailed as the phone rang again.

By Tuesday afternoon, the answer to that question was Rachel. She had spent two days on an emotional roller coaster, anxiously awaiting a summons from senior management about her part in Friday's chaos yet revelling in Jeremy's unceremonious departure. His offending email had circulated throughout TAG, eliciting many expressions of support for her that mitigated her embarrassment at his slighting remarks. She could hardly believe that her wish for him to disappear had been answered so quickly, and due to his own idiocy. When she was called to see the deputy director, she still half-expected to be reprimanded for her part in the gala's mess and was relieved to discover that John laid no blame on her shoulders. Stunned, she accepted his offer to replace Jeremy as acting head.

Her first day in her new role had been long and tiring, as she careened from meeting to meeting. Jeremy had always seemed busy, but he had left a daunting number of tasks incomplete, from urgent items like the interpretive video for the Ramsay exhibition to critical ones like drafting the department's budget. She stayed up late on Wednesday night, finishing a report for development and writing the agenda for the departmental meeting the next morning.

Jeremy is gone. You know the job. Blow them away. Yes, Nick. She felt today's meeting would be crucial in establishing her authority and forming a rapport with the coordinators. Given its importance, she regretted that she'd only begun to think about what she'd say at the meeting at eleven last night, and she wished she'd snagged a few more hours of sleep before she had to face her unruly subordinates.

Rachel booted up her computer, found the agenda she had emailed from home, opened it, and clicked print. She made her way to the shared printer, nestled in the back near the cubicles of Samantha and the other interpretive planners. As she approached, she heard Sam's raised voice.

"I won't take it!"

Uh-oh. Post-Jeremy blues? So much for a great meeting. She gathered up the copies of the agenda, then looked over the wall. Samantha's face, framed by blond curls, had turned a furious pink.

"What's the matter, Sam?" Rachel asked. "Anything I can help with?"

"It's my label," Samantha said. "Amanda's rejected it. Again."

"Oh, I see," said Rachel, not seeing at all. "Maybe you'd better come to my office so we can talk about it."

Once seated, with the door closed, Samantha explained.

"Amanda has this new work by Pedro Havilio that she wants to install pretty soon. I worked really hard on the label for it, but Amanda keeps rejecting it and sending me back this art jargon that nobody will understand! It's awful. And she's over the word limit. Jeremy was really strict about sixty words and that's what mine is. I can't take it anymore."

"Anymore? Has this happened before?" Rachel asked.

"Yeah," said Samantha, her eyes watering. "I always get a lot of grief, but this time is the worst. It's horrible. 'Proto-real, hyper-actual'! What does that even mean? She said I had to learn how theory informs contemporary art, otherwise I'd just continue reducing the meaning to one-syllable words and never write anything worth reading. And she sent it to you too." She looked at Rachel resentfully.

"When was this?"

"Yesterday morning."

Rachel remembered she had seen an email from Amanda but hadn't opened it, as she had so many more pressing issues that required her attention.

"Hmmm," she said, turning to her computer. She quickly found Amanda's email and opened up the attachment. She scanned the re-written label text, recognizing the curator's style from her first year at the gallery. Contemporary labels had definitely become more accessible once the planners took over writing them.

Samantha looked defiantly at Rachel. "Jeremy was pretty clear that he had the final say, which means you. Now. If you won't back me, I'll quit."

Rachel stared at her, eyes wide. First major challenge, but she detected a reassuring quaver in Samantha's voice. She took a deep breath and asked, "When's the work being installed?"

"Two weeks."

"Okay, so we have some time. Sam, I'm sorry you're so upset, and I'm sorry that I didn't see this yesterday, but I've been pretty busy. Maybe you could send me your version of the label and I'll look at it after the meeting. I'm sure we can sort something out."

Samantha stood up. "I can't work here if I have to write like that. Jeremy would never stand for this."

"Right," said Rachel. "Thanks for clarifying that. I'll see you in the meeting."

Labels. She'd heard it called the Armageddon of museum work, which seemed exaggerated to an outsider until one realized the investment of each side in the interpretation of a work of art. And that was before the public chimed in. The process of transferring the label-writing job from curators to educators had been a fractious one. Stinger always made it sound like his greater understanding of the visitor had convinced the curators to release this important work to him and his staff, but Rachel had heard a few rumblings that suggested it wasn't a *fait accompli*. And now it landed in her lap. Thanks, Jeremy.

She looked at the pile of agendas on her desk, thinking of the people she would face around the table. Most of the staff had been hired within the past two years. In the five months that Jeremy had managed the department, she felt it had not cohered in a satisfying way: each section carried on like a little fiefdom, doing its job, while Jeremy promoted interpretive planning. Rachel wondered if she would lose all hope of gaining the head position if she burned herself out trying to unite them. That could be her Armageddon. Then she gave herself a mental shake, thinking that Nick would surely reproach her for such hyperbole. *You know the job. Blow them away.* He may have said those words out of frustration with her fretting, but they could serve as her armour as she headed into battle. *Along with coffee*, she thought, yawning. She definitely needed a coffee. Thank goodness she still had time to get one from the café.

Fifteen minutes later, Rachel walked into the meeting room. To her surprise, Naomi was already there, turning away from the notice board. They had not spoken since Monday morning, each content to avoid the other after Jeremy's dismissal. Rachel had overheard Naomi proclaiming TAG Camp's success to the team, despite the chaos it had caused. With a smug smile, the family programs coordinator trotted to a chair at the far end of the table. Rachel turned toward the notice board to find one item: a photograph. When Rachel stepped closer to examine it, she almost dropped her coffee. Damn, that gala photographer didn't miss a trick. He had perfectly framed the grand staircase as Damian leapt up one side and naturists descended the other. Right in the middle was Rachel herself, gaping in mid-dash.

Rachel tore the picture off the board and glared at Naomi. "Where did you get this?"

"From the photo department. I selected a few of the best photos from the TAG Camp so marketing can, like, pursue a sponsor. It's such a great program." Naomi sat down with a hair toss. "I couldn't help but notice some of the photos he shot at the gala. I thought everyone would want to see what went on. So that's what you call, like, managing a tour, Rachel?" Her disingenuous tone slid into a sneer.

Rachel flushed as she slammed the photo on top of the agendas on the table. *What a cheeky upstart*, she thought, channelling her grandmother. *Sorry, gran, but that's too sedate for Naomi.* Much as Rachel hated to call anyone a bitch, that seemed the most applicable word for her annoying colleague. She'd had enough of her flouncing, her prancing, her hair-tossing, and her smugness. "In case you haven't read the deputy director's email, Jeremy was fired last Monday and I'm the acting head now. I'll thank you not to undermine me."

"You couldn't even keep those naturists together! You let them wander all over the place."

"You disobeyed Jeremy's orders and let the kids run into the mezzanine. And you kept the kids upstairs past eight. You should not have been there. Don't say that I let the naturists run wild. It's not true."

"But—"

"I want you to understand something. Jeremy's move into management made it easy to fire him. You are still in the union. I may not be able terminate your employment, but I *can* reprimand you. There's a disciplinary process I could go through with HR to deal with your behaviour. You deliberately disrupted the assigned schedule by keeping the kids upstairs past eight, and then you let the kids run down the staircase. Completely irresponsible, not to mention unsafe."

"It was the TV people. They wanted to see everything. I didn't want them to leave. I don't know, I guess the kids were, like, excited, and ran into the mezzanine to take a peek at what was happening. What's the problem?"

"It disturbed a very important event! Your lack of control of your group is a serious breach of your professional responsibility."

Naomi's eye widened. Good, that shut her up.

After a deep breath, Rachel said, "Like it or not, I'm your boss now. You have no business posting this photograph, and I refuse to put up with you trying to shame and undermine me in front of the others. We've got to establish some way of working together."

Naomi swallowed hard. "Everyone's against me in this department. The only person who supported me was Jeremy."

Rachel noticed her bottom lip quivering and took heart from this crack in Naomi's defensive, irritating, egotistical shell. "That's not true," she said. "Family programs are just as important as any other area. That's the point. They're all equal. Jeremy might have led you to think otherwise, but he's gone. That doesn't mean your area is threatened. But you've got to get down off your high horse and start being a team player."

Naomi clenched her lips and allowed herself a glance at Rachel.

"It's okay if you don't like me," Rachel continued. "We don't have to like each other to work together." Naomi's eyes widened and Rachel felt a rush at finally being able to voice the words she'd wanted to say forever. "Look, I've got to pull all the program plans for the Ramsay exhibition together in the next few weeks. I'm sure your plans for the family programs space are terrific. I'm counting on you to make education look good. That's all I want. I think that's all we all want." She kept up her placating tone, hoping to quell the other's volatility.

"Are you still going to, like, go to HR about me?"

"I'll think about it. Senior management are examining the events of Friday night. They've spoken to me, and they may speak to you. We all want the record set straight. But I don't want to get our new working relationship off to a rough start, so promise me you'll think about what I've said."

"Okay," Naomi said. *Not very graciously*, Rachel thought, *but good enough for a start*. Then Naomi stood, picked up her folder, and headed toward the door. "I know marketing will, like, support me. They love my program," she said defiantly.

Good grief, thought Rachel, channelling Arthur. Did Naomi hear anything she'd said? She turned to find the rest of the department blocking the doorway of the conference room, waiting to enter. They parted briefly to allow Naomi to barge through, then filtered into the room and sat down, regarding her warily.

"I'm sorry you had to hear that," she said, her face reddening, avoiding their eyes as she pushed the agendas down the centre of the table. "I'm sure Naomi will return, but we'll start the meeting without her." She almost hoped she didn't. At least she could trust this bunch to behave like adults.

The studio coordinator broke the awkward silence. "Rachel, how could we ever carry on without Naomi? She might just dream up a new program … like TAG Tots!"

Everyone snickered. Rachel thought, recalling last Friday's VIP tour, that another program possibility could be TAG Tits. But she kept that to herself as she savoured the break in the tension. Key moment. Set the tone. "We'll save program proposals for another meeting. Let's start with reports. School programs first."

Naomi pranced in a few minutes later, holding a pile of photographs. *Here comes the full-on TAG Camp apotheosis*, thought Rachel. In spite of her determination to run a tight meeting, she let herself get momentarily distracted by an image of Naomi on a hilltop, eyes looking heavenward, hair flying in the wind, a horde of costumed kids shining flashlights up at her.

Well, at least she came back.

Around six, Rachel abandoned her overflowing desk to join Tina at Buzz's Pub, the favourite after-work watering hole for a segment of TAG's staff. Senior managers never ventured into its dim ambience, where beer logos and music posters graced the walls above the dark brown panelling. Cheap beer, salty food, two pool tables, and proximity to the gallery attracted staff from exhibitions, education, and junior administration. Two of the installation technicians played pool near a table of their colleagues while the visitor services department ordered jugs of draft at another. Indie rock music, a feature of Buzz's eclectic taste, drifted from the speakers, loud enough to signal the workday had ended, soft enough to encourage the mutual griping that never did.

"Cheers," said Tina. "You've been under Stinger's shadow for too long. Now that even George knows he's a prick, it's time to show what you can do. TAG, you're it!"

"You must have been pretty busy too," said Rachel, "unless Kristen sorted out all the bad press the gallery got this week." She knew that would unleash a scornful retort from Tina about her boss, one of a long line of marketing heads who exhibited frenetic energy but came to rely on Tina's stable competence.

Tina snorted. "Fat chance! First, she's on a high because Naomi told her that sleepover thing went superbly, so she's picturing all sorts of great marketing spinoffs. Then she had to chew out Gary for not showing up when I had to leave. He was supposed to escort the TV crew until eight, but he mixed up the dates."

"Of all the days for him to get wrong!"

Tina rolled her eyes. "I don't think it's hit Kristen that we have some serious PR repair to do. Even with the Avalon Dance Company."

Rachel raised her eyebrows. "What are they upset about?"

"Their leader had a hissy fit with the special events staff. She was pissed off that the kids were laughing and running around, and then with that Damian's appearance on the landing. It distracted the guests. Apparently, she told them we have no respect for artists and she won't dance here again."

"'No respect for artists.' That's a great slogan for TAG!" laughed Rachel.

Tina continued her tale of the ups and downs of marketing and communications in the post-gala week, ending with, "It's a wonder we got that media announcement about Drake's donation out at all."

"I think I read that," said Rachel, trying to recall it from the blizzard of emails she'd received. "Any response?"

"Yeah. A couple of journalists want to interview him, so I'm arranging those."

"I thought Kristen liked to handle the VIPs."

"She does, but there's just so much coming at us. She's losing it. I pretty much took over and sorted out all the calls and told her what we were doing. She actually said thank you." Tina widened her eyes in mock astonishment.

"Uh-oh. Watch out or she might realize that you run the department."

Tina shrugged. "So what. I'm not ambitious enough to want to be a senior manager. Let her attend all those meetings. I'm just fine where I am." They both sipped their beer. "You know, I really get a kick out of Kinsella's articles. I loved the line about birthday suits being the new dress code. He says what we'd like to, if we didn't have to polish everything to make George Caldwell look like the greatest museum director ever. But how are you doing? I bet you've more than filled Stinger's shoes."

Rachel gave a rundown of her two days on the job, highlighting the clash with Naomi. A platter of gooey nachos arrived, and Tina tucked into them while she listened. She pulled a chip away from the platter to stretch out the cheese, broke the strand with her other hand, and expertly twirled it around before she ate it. Growing hungrier as she watched Tina devour a few of those, Rachel paused to eat a chip loaded with olives and sour cream.

"That Naomi's a piece of work," said Tina. "She'll have to adjust to a world without Stinger now."

"Right. And then I had a meeting with financial! He hauled me up to chew me out about the budget. The latest statement shows this deficit of twenty thousand dollars, and he asked me how I planned to eradicate it. I pointed out to him that as I've just been appointed acting head, and this was the first I knew of it. Of course I had no idea how to resolve it."

"Twenty thousand? That would be par for the course in the curatorial area, but it seems like a lot in education," said Tina. "Have you figured it out?"

"Of course, Tina. You know my talent for looking at numbers, that's why I studied art history." Rachel rolled her eyes while Tina snickered. "Part of it comes from those artists' talks I ran last year. The attendance was uneven, and they didn't meet the expected revenue."

"Well, you know what they say about artists' talks: if they made money, Walmart would be doing them."

Rachel almost spat out a mouthful of beer as she laughed. "Maybe I'll make that my slogan. Put it on my bulletin board." She explained some of the anomalies she'd found, that implied that Jeremy had overspent on the Museum Summit and several other projects.

"I'm still looking. There's no way they'll pin any over-spending on me. Or make me lay off staff to deal with it. It never seems to be curatorial or administration or human resources who lose staff, but departments like education."

"And then there's a restructuring and a round of new hirings ten months later," said Tina. "To paraphrase Warhol's over-used line, I think that, in the future, everyone will work at TAG for fifteen minutes." They laughed.

Tina scooped up a chip. "I know you want to apply for the head job, but between Naomi and the budget, I'll bet it doesn't look so sweet."

Rachel shrugged. "I knew there'd be headaches. Oh! That reminds me. I had this crazy dream last night, where I was standing in the middle of a circle and all these people were shining flashlights on me. Naomi, Sam, Jeremy, other staff, the naturists, parents, Amanda. Even docents and teachers and visitors. And I was nude!" She shook her head in mock self-pity. "Nobody knows what an acting head of education has to endure." She chased a drop of salsa around the platter with a chip.

Tina laughed. "Tales of mountain rescue pale by comparison! But why was Amanda there?"

Rachel finished chewing her chip. "I had to battle her on behalf of the planners."

Tina raised her eyebrows. "What happened?" She nodded at the waiter who asked if they wanted another round. Rachel told her about Samantha's ultimatum over her rewritten Havilio label.

"So, I reviewed the guidelines for label-writing, which, to Jeremy's credit, he got the curators to agree to. I decided Sam's label was fine. It was clear and it met the word limit. I sent an email to Amanda telling her that, and I copied Roger. He's her boss, after all."

"You wouldn't know it, by the way she goes straight to George all the time," said Tina. "How did she respond?"

"She agreed. Or rather, she said she didn't have time to debate art language with me, so she let it go."

"Here's to you," said Tina, raising her glass. "She came down from Planet Curator." That was the name they had coined to explain the inexplicable behaviour of curators.

At that moment, Justin sauntered over from the pool table with his beer and sat down. He wore his Support Canadian Artists Now T-shirt.

"You caused a ruckus on Friday," said Rachel. "Or rather added to it."

Justin shrugged. "We have a right to protest. It was lucky that that TV crew was there. Simon Kinsella too."

"How did you know that the commission was going to an American artist?" asked Tina.

"Can't reveal our sources," said Justin with a smile. Tina and Rachel looked at each other knowingly. He had all but confirmed Amanda's role.

"Do you think your protest will have an effect?"

"Someone in the director's office told me they've been getting lots of calls, so yeah. Kinsella's article helped."

"I bet they're getting calls about all sorts of fallout from Friday." Then Rachel remembered something. "I have a bone to pick with you, Justin."

He looked at her over his beer glass.

"Why wasn't that bust of Miss Littlewood fastened to the pedestal? I had to go way beyond my job description to save it from tumbling down the stairs last Friday. It might have hurt a patron!"

Justin grinned. "Uh, yeah, sorry about that, Rachel. Our boss wasn't too happy either when he called me to go in on Saturday. It's those damn Brodeur cameras. The bust had been removed for cleaning and I brought it back first thing on Friday morning. I set it on the pedestal, then I got called away to fix the camera in the nineteenth-century gallery. It's the hardest to reach. We were short-staffed and just never got back to the bust. Good thing it was only like that for a day."

"And who would expect some yoga guru to wrap his arms around it!" said Tina.

"Bare arms, as I heard," said Justin. "He must be a real art buff."

"Puh-lease," Rachel groaned. "I've had enough nudist puns for one week."

One of his colleagues called him back to the pool table.

"I wonder how Justin likes leading a double life," said Tina. "That department likes to hire artists because they're so meticulous with the works, but he's kind of a subversive too."

"He's definitely got an axe to grind against TAG."

"So how much work do you have to do for the Ramsay exhibition?" Rachel started explaining the various projects that had fallen into her lap and forgot about Justin. She realized that she felt good talking about her work and looked forward to the next three weeks. Lots to do, but she had already dreamt the worst. Things couldn't get too bad if she could keep her clothes on.

CHAPTER 27
AMANDA

On Thursday evening, Amanda relaxed on the cream-coloured sofa in her lakeside condo, thinking over the information gained in a call to London that morning. When the name Hathaway rang that bell on Friday, she had determined to speak to an old university friend who worked in an auction house in that city. His familiarity with the market for pre-1900 works of art proved very useful. She could hardly wait to tell Steven about it when he arrived shortly.

This news buoyed her up after the gala's fallout, a mixed result for her. In spite of her anger at George over the announcement about the sculpture commission going to Daniel Reid, and her awareness that the gala's demise did not bode well for TAG, she was pleased that Justin's collective had stirred up resistance in the Toronto art world. Her department's phones had rung constantly this week and she had received many supportive emails that decried the gallery's decision. She had to choose her words carefully in responding to those who assumed she had agreed to the choice; she was more grateful to the correspondents who commiserated with her over George's heavy-handed management.

At her desk that morning, Amanda reflected that she still hadn't heard a complete explanation for Friday's mess, although she gathered the naturists had something to do with Arthur and that Ramsay show. Such a shambles would never happen with her donors. Any concern for Arthur quickly dropped as she faced the many tasks before her. Friday's pledge count had not reached the target, so development warned her that she might have to make some calls.

She hardly needed that addition to her plate, but she knew that department was desperately trying to transform the campaign's calamitous launch into a seaworthy vessel. *Good luck*, she thought, but agreed to do what she could.

An email from the exhibitions head told her some new works were being collected earlier than planned, so she had a few new objects to check on. She knew that her assistant had an interview with an art magazine about a group show of Indigenous artists in the first-floor contemporary galleries. Amanda wanted to make sure the journalist spoke to her as well, to hear her statement about the growing diversity in her exhibition planning, aimed at dispelling the many criticisms directed at the gallery for its hitherto Eurocentric approach. She sighed, feeling nobody understood the difficult lot of a contemporary art curator. Sometimes she saw herself slaloming through an obstacle course, head down to avoid barbs from artists, critics, freelance curators, the media, board trustees, and members. She almost envied Roger and Arthur for toiling safely in the realm of dead artists, where complaining wasn't an option. Almost. She didn't envy Arthur much right now.

That reminded her of Simone Brodeur. One of the patrons at Friday night's gala owned a piece by Simone and let her know of the announcement about Daniel Reid, which provoked a strained-sounding voicemail message on Monday. Amanda had yet to answer it. She didn't think that Simone had told her patron, or anyone else, of their fateful chat, but she still felt guilty for having raised the artist's hopes. She owed her an apology and an explanation, but hated to admit that George pulled the rug out from under her.

In the afternoon, Amanda dispensed with Rachel's email about the Havilio label, then had to endure an equally irritating one from the exhibitions head:

I regret to tell you that your request for ten brushed-steel cases for the Havilio piece, custom-made with non-reflective plexi, cannot be met. As I only received it a week ago, and there's no budget for it, we'll proceed with our plan to reuse ten very serviceable white cases.

Amanda sighed, then decided that she had larger issues to fight for, so unwillingly replied with a terse agreement.

Now, as she poured a glass of red wine, Amanda's thoughts were far from the petty irritations of over-simplified educators' labels and penny-pinching exhibitions managers. She mulled over her early morning conversation, which confirmed what she'd picked up at curatorial meetings: Lionel Hathaway, a London dealer specializing in eighteenth-century paintings, was one to avoid. In a scathing tone, her friend had denounced Hathaway's unethical mix of dealing and appraising. A Hathaway appraisal often proved to be questionably high, so his auction house always did a double check on works that had passed through his hands.

She could imagine Victor Drake dropping his wife off at Harrods, then walking along Knightsbridge and Piccadilly to Hathaway's gallery on some little side street. Amanda speculated that there weren't many eighteenth-century horse paintings left to sell, but if the dealer had a sideline in endorsing exaggerated appraisals for clients, that could prove lucrative and keep him in business.

She and Steven hadn't been together in two weeks due to his business travel and family commitments, and she missed him. Their quick embrace in the gallery last Friday reinforced that. He rang the intercom at six thirty and she leapt to buzz him in. After a long kiss, they settled on the couch. A little different from earlier days, when they would have headed straight for the bedroom, but Amanda felt they could take their time. She was too curious to learn how Steven had handled her request for help to check out Victor.

"You looked great, by the way," said Steven, clinking his glass against hers. "Last Friday."

"Oh, thanks. It's always a treat to have a new dress. I like to look good when my boss dumps on me in public."

"Is Daniel Reid that bad?"

"He's not bad at all. He's terrific. And he's a hot name right now, which I think is the appeal for George. No, it's the principle of the thing. George shouldn't be overriding me."

"I agree, especially if you've already spoken to an artist about it."

"Oh, forget I told you about her. I'm trying to forget I approached her." Amanda sipped her wine to assuage the guilty twinge she felt at not having returned Simone's call. "This is not my favourite topic. I'd rather talk about Victor Drake. Any scoop?"

Steven raised his eyebrows.

"You're in luck. I had lunch yesterday with a couple of guys who know him. They had heard about last Friday's event, so we got onto Victor quite easily. I don't think they're his best friends."

"Do tell." Amanda curled her legs underneath her and leaned toward Steven.

"He's successful, he's ruthless, you know, typical businessman stuff. He loves his horses. He hates paying taxes. The other guys were ticked off at how often Victor has boasted about getting his accountant, or whoever, to reduce his taxes to nothing. Apparently he's the king of write-offs. That's all legal. He just knows how to take advantage of the right loopholes."

"No surprise there. Anything illegal?"

"Well, they're not sure how he got the zoning rights for his latest mall. The land was zoned residential for a long time, then suddenly when Victor acquired it, it changed. Nobody mentioned bribes, but they said it seemed murky."

"Hmmm. Well, tax avoidance rings true," said Amanda. "That bolsters what I learned today." She told Steven about the folder she'd seen on George's desk and her subsequent chat with the London auctioneer.

"So you think Victor's paying this guy to give a high appraisal for his collection?"

"I can't see a need for Hathaway letterhead to be on the director's desk unless George is pursuing an appraisal. There has to be some connection with Victor's donation." Amanda finished her wine and placed the glass on the coffee table. She turned to Steven and laced her arms around his neck. "Well done."

"If the reward is what I think it is, I'll snoop for you anytime." He put down his glass as Amanda laughed.

FRIDAY

CHAPTER 28
GEORGE

George slammed down the telephone receiver and glared at Amanda as his assistant shut the door. All week he had laboured non-stop on repairing last Friday's damages and cajoling gala attendees, with little result yet. Victor, to his relief, had marshalled his persuasive powers to convince a few of them to support the gallery. He hoped that progress would dim the chairman's interest in questioning his own fitness for his job. They were meeting soon for lunch to compare notes. Amanda was the last person he wanted to see at the end of a stressful week, especially when she wore such an unfriendly expression.

"Is it urgent?"

"Yes, it's urgent." Without waiting for an invitation, Amanda sat across from him.

"I've got fifteen minutes."

"Thank you for making the time," she said with a note of sarcasm. "I've been wanting to talk to you about an important issue."

"Oh? What's that?"

"Your very close relationship with Victor Drake and the dealer Lionel Hathaway." George bolted upright in his chair. Damn. He should have known she'd be trouble. The chairman had continued to harp on about using Hathaway for the second appraisal, testing George's patience as he tried to focus on the campaign. He wondered what the hell she knew.

"What are you talking about?"

"I think you know, George. I'm talking about the fact that Lionel Hathaway has a lucrative sideline in providing inflated assessments of the value of works of art. I don't know if he's providing the first or second appraisal for Victor's donation, but I'm sure the only reason you're consulting with him is to help procure the highest possible tax credit. No doubt the promise of obtaining such a credit has motivated our philanthropic" — Amanda emphasized this word in a way that annoyed George — "chairman to make such a hefty pledge to your building campaign. Which, of course, gets him another tax credit. Quite the mutually satisfying arrangement."

George swallowed hard, then tightened his jaw, perplexed as to how the hell she had figured it out. "You've got a bloody nerve to imply that I would engage in any illegal or questionable proceedings around a donation," he blustered. "Or that anyone else would. It's Roger's job to oversee such applications for European art. You're insinuating—"

"Then why is paperwork from Hathaway in your office?" Amanda folded her arms and surveyed George. "Of course, it's Roger's job to oversee that application. I can't imagine him agreeing to an appraisal from a shady character like Hathaway."

Damn it, thought George. What does she want? Amanda took a breath and continued.

"You're overstepping your authority by meddling in European curatorial matters, just like you did when you gave that commission to Daniel Reid."

So that's what this is about. She's angry enough about that to go after him. She must have seen his Hathaway folder. He pushed his chair back, a bad move as his knee flared up. Ouch! He really had to start doing his exercises. Bending slightly to rub it, he avoided Amanda's eyes.

"You're overstepping your authority with your insinuations about my management practices, not to mention my ethics," he said.

"I say insinuations, because you have no proof of any of this. I'm not impressed by your eagerness to impugn both Victor and me in underhanded dealings. It's only natural that we work closely together, as he fully supports me in the campaign. As I expect all staff to do. And" — he remembered his own trump card, a disk produced from security's video surveillance — "I think you have your own close relationship that merits questioning." Amanda's eyes flickered.

"I'm sure you're aware that all our galleries have video surveillance? And, of course, those cameras were on the night of the gala. Even in the nineteenth-century gallery, which nobody had any reason to enter. Except you, apparently."

It was Amanda's turn to gulp.

"You and Steven Katz, according to this tape. You two look very close."

George savoured the signs of embarrassment — red face, darting eyes — that confirmed his suspicions about her relationship with Katz.

"Amanda, I don't give a shit about my staff's personal lives. You can fuck whomever you want, married or not. But don't get moralistic with me. You were caught on the recording camera. How does that look, curators meeting their lovers for supposedly private trysts?"

Amanda's right hand flew to her mouth for a moment, then lowered as she glared at George.

"Well, at least I wasn't putting on a show for the *Gestes* camera. I heard about you losing your cool in there later. There was quite a crowd outside watching as it was projected."

"I suppose you heard about that from your artist friends?" George suddenly remembered that the spokesman for the protest was one of TAG's installation technicians. "I'd like to know how they heard so quickly about the commission going to Reid."

Amanda tossed her hair as if his semi-accusation had nothing to do with her, but he noted with satisfaction that she swallowed hard. She must have fed that ragtag mob the information. He let his comment hang in the air while he reverted to his own defence.

"If I didn't have such incompetent staff screwing up the gala, I wouldn't have had to blow up. How did I know the Ramsays were going to burst in?" George spun in his chair to one side but that provided a better view of the smashed model, reminding him of another weak moment. He swung back to face Amanda, who still looked uneasy under her defiant veneer, and decided he had more leverage over her.

"So now I know one of my curators is having an affair with a married collector, while she has the temerity to make wild accusations about my behaviour," said George. "Not a very secure position for you, unless…"

"Unless?" asked Amanda, her hands clutching the chair arms.

"The campaign needs some help. Steven Katz is a rich developer, and I haven't seen a pledge from him yet. As a member of the Gold Leaf Circle and a collector of contemporary art, nurtured, I assume, by your expert guidance" — Amanda stayed impassive as George emphasized that phrase — "Steven should be willing to support the Toronto Art Gallery. For at least five million."

Amanda clenched her jaw and crossed her legs and arms as she assessed her situation. George glanced at his watch.

"I can do better than that, George. If I can get a patron, or patrons, to fund the commission by an artist of my choosing, and donate to the campaign, you get rid of that disk. And I'll forget that Lionel Hathaway has any relation to this gallery." She sat back and looked at George, chin lifted.

George raised his eyebrows and stood up. He paced to the window. Amanda's pitch impressed him. She didn't have to know about his own misgivings regarding Lionel Hathaway. But Zach was still a problem. He couldn't just ditch him, as that would upset Victor. He swung back to look at Amanda, who was half-turned toward him.

"I think you're crossing boundaries, Amanda. It's not my practice to drop generous patrons who are enlightened enough to fund a commission." He ignored the soft snort that Amanda made as he heaped praise on Zach. He knew he was piling it on, but he took enough bullying from his father; he didn't need it from her too. "The campaign is my priority now. When I see a pledge from Steven Katz, I'll get rid of the recording."

"But what about Hathaway? I'll bet Simon Kinsella would love to know about him."

Amanda stood up to face the director, as if to prevent him looming over her.

"I'm sure he'd love to know about curators' private lives too," said George, swinging back to his chair. She was scared. And he was the director. "Like I said, the campaign's the priority. Get me five million, and we'll see where we stand."

Amanda stood with her hands on her hips, glaring at George.

"I understand. The campaign's the priority." She marched out of the office.

George leaned back in his chair. The saying "keep your friends close and your enemies closer" drifted across his mind as he pictured himself confronting a firing squad again. Everyone he dealt with took a turn in each category. Should he have seen this coming? As he twisted his ring around his finger he thought, not for the first time, how little he knew about his staff. Trust Amanda to have a network that reached into the world of dealers of eighteenth-century British art. He wondered how soon he'd hear about Katz's campaign pledge. And how he could get Victor to drop the unsavoury Hathaway.

George rose to walk down to a steakhouse on King Street that was near Victor's headquarters, relieved to get out of his office, where the smashed model and ever-ringing phones reminded him of all the recovery work he had to do. As he passed the *Gestes* projection outside, now innocently depicting a school group in the sculpture gallery, he thought back to Monday when he had chewed out the marketing head for arranging for those cameras to stay on. And then that bloody TV cameraman had caught the action outside. This gallery had too many cameras! At least the security cameras had proved useful to help put Amanda in her place.

George blinked as he left the April sunshine for the dimmer ambience of the restaurant, one of the chairman's favourites. He thought that the dark wood-panelled walls and red leather banquettes doubtless flattered Victor's self-image as a leader in business and now cultural philanthropy. Walking across the bustling room, alive with noon-time business chatter, he noticed that Victor, instead of displaying the boldness of the hunter, bagging malls, horses, and paintings with equal voracity, looked uneasy.

After ordering a Perrier, George said, "I've got some good news from development. Our calls have brought in some donations. Setting up the big model and the drawings in the lobby helps to keep the campaign highly visible. We're up to ten million now."

"Hmmph. Not exactly where we wanted to be, is it? What about those Ramsays? They didn't seem too happy with your gallery last Friday."

George paused as the waiter came to take their orders. He had managed to keep his faux pas secret from Victor, who knew nothing of the cancelled pick-up. With the delivery re-booked for next week, that crisis was over and he intended to convey that he was still in charge of "his" gallery, as his chairman so affectionately referred to it. Hiding his irritation, he opted for flattery. "They're fine. Minor misunderstanding. Thanks for all your hard work, Victor. You've brought in some sizable pledges. We couldn't do this campaign without you."

"I'm proud to say I can provide some good coverage for the gallery. *Caledon Life*'s publishing my interview next week. They came to the farm to photograph me with the horses. Should be a good spread."

"That's great."

"Great? It's more than great, George. There's another one coming out in the *Gazette* soon. It's all good promotion for the new wing." *Not to mention your horses, your business, and your collection,* thought George.

Victor pushed a large white envelope across the table. "Here's the paperwork."

"Thanks," said George, pulling out the signed pledge form for Victor's campaign donation. Ten million in the bag. "Development will love to see this." He put the paper back into the envelope and set it to one side. "But you seem preoccupied. You're not still going to call a board meeting about me, are you?" George said it with a smile, somehow sensing that Victor's unease had nothing to do with questioning his directorial competence.

"Board meeting? No, no," said Victor, shifting his thickset bulk and frowning at a corner of the table. "But I am worried. It's about Zach."

"Oh? What's up?" George's skepticism about Zach surfaced, a skepticism he had hidden from Victor so far. Getting a donor to fund a big commission had been irresistible, but possibly hasty.

"He's been preoccupied lately. We met yesterday. His business isn't doing as well as I thought. Or as he let me think," said Victor, a note of bitterness creeping into his voice. "In fact, he's in serious trouble."

"I see. I'm sorry to hear that. I imagine it's a disappointment for you, Victor, and I hope Zach can turn things around, but what...?"

"What does it mean for the commission?" Victor took out a white handkerchief and dabbed his sweating forehead. *He's really upset*, thought George. He had never seen him like this. "He can't bloody pay for it, that's what it means. He should never have agreed to it in the first place."

George watched the older man press his handkerchief against his upper lip as he shook his head, eyes fixed on the floor. George almost felt sorry for him, as he appreciated Victor's pride in his business-minded son. Almost. Now he cursed himself for ever having trusted Victor's elevation of Zach to art patron. He would have to find another funder for the Reid commission, unless Amanda came through. How she'd love to hear this conversation.

"I see," said George, considering his words carefully. "I'm sure we can find another patron. And we still have your generous support."

"Yes, of course," said Victor, raising his head and putting away his handkerchief. "That's why I wanted to tell you myself. We've got a good relationship, so I thought this bad news might be easier to take coming from me.

"I appreciate that." George paused as their meals arrived. The chairman had not raised the Lionel Hathaway appraisal issue in the past few days, but George sensed that would not last. The news about Zach and apparent disinterest in firing him shifted leverage his way, so he decided to test just how good their relationship was.

"Have you lined up Hathaway for the appraisal yet?" Victor asked, holding his knife and fork as if about to carve up George instead of his steak.

The moment had arrived. "No, and I'm not going to."

"What? I insist that you use him! Haven't I been telling you that? Goddammit, don't you want my collection?" spluttered Victor, his face flushing.

"Of course, I want your collection. And your donation," George said calmly, neatly slicing his knife through his grilled lamb chop. "But unfortunately your choice of appraiser is a problem. To put it bluntly, he has a sleazy reputation because of his inflated evaluations. I'm going to ask Roger to find another reputable one. If they don't agree with your first appraisal, you're going to have to settle for the lower tax credit. That's not the end of the world."

"What the hell? That's no way to treat a donor. What kind of half-assed gallery do you run?"

"Actually, I run a professional public art gallery and we don't engage in unethical procedures. You will still get a tax credit for donating your paintings, based on their worth when you bought them."

"I don't like paying more taxes than I have to. Let me call Hathaway."

"No. If you want to remain chair of the board, and chair of the TAG21 campaign, and keep your status as a cultural philanthropist, you'll back down on this and let us handle your collection properly. And I won't make a big deal about Zach's sudden withdrawal of his patronage."

If disbelief and outrage could be vaporized, George would have seen steam puffing out of Victor's ears. The older man glared at him, tight-lipped for several moments, then looked down.

"Okay, okay. Do it your way."

"Right," said George. He finished cutting his first piece of lamb and ate it. Contrary to the chairman's view, George felt relieved that he'd dispensed with the unpleasant spectre of Lionel Hathaway and did not see Zach's departure as negative. No need to tell Amanda about it while she was presumably trying to find her own funder. He put thoughts of her and Zach aside as his donor relations training kicked in. "Victor, we're a great team. I know we can get the campaign back on track. Our campaign. Who do you think we should approach next?"

Victor looked at George soulfully while he chewed his steak, then smiled. "I've got a good bet."

THREE WEEKS
LATER, FRIDAY

CHAPTER 29
RACHEL

"Thank you! I'm so honoured." Rachel barely absorbed what the director of the university art gallery went on to say, so surprised and excited was she by the news.

"I understand, but can I please have the weekend to think it over?" Having gained that assurance, she put the receiver down and gazed into space. The education area hummed with the usual activity of a Friday morning — docents arriving for their tours, school coordinators conferring over the schedule, the receptionist fielding calls — but she didn't notice any of it as she processed what she had just heard. She had been offered the job of head of programs at the university art gallery.

The past three and a half weeks had been so hectic due to her post-Jeremy promotion that her interview, though not forgotten, had receded to the back of her mind. Advancing from her previous self-image as a worker bee, Rachel saw herself as a beaver, diligently damming the torrent of jobs. She bustled from meetings to emails to helping hire artists for the summer programs to many tasks related to the Ramsay exhibition. She wrote the exhibition brochure, proofed its design, and spent hours in the editing suite with the media producer consulting on the contextual video that Jeremy had barely started. Putting in long hours, Rachel barely noticed any preparations going on outside education, grateful for the fact that everyone seemed to grapple with their jobs, while she swung from the intellectually and artistically engaging tasks of working on the exhibition to the more mundane ones of struggling to comprehend the department's finances and deflecting impatient reminders from human resources about overdue performance assessments. The members' opening for the Ramsay exhibition was that evening, so, with deadlines met, she had a hiatus in which to consider her future. She called Nick to tell him her good news, then read the *Tribune*'s review.

Successful Trails and Donor Trials at TAG

Simon Kinsella

Arts Reporter

Terrain and Town: The Ramsay Canadian Collection is a must-see exhibition at the Toronto Art Gallery, opening to the public tomorrow and running until October 25. Curator Arthur Matlock presents paintings by important Canadian artists of the late-19th and early-20th-centuries, who worked mainly in eastern Ontario and Quebec. While some names, like Charles Talbot and Émile Legrande, will be familiar to art-lovers, most are lesser known.

"We're very proud to be presenting the Ramsay collection for the first time," stated George Caldwell, director. "These stellar works of Canadian art are an important addition to our national art history and we are very grateful to the Ramsay Foundation for its generous support of the exhibition."

The article cited paintings by five different artists, with several punchy quotes from Arthur elucidating their style, subject matter, and importance to Canadian art history. Kinsella lamented the low number of female artists in the exhibition but praised the work of the two represented. After recommending the well-illustrated catalogue, he gave a rare nod to education by mentioning that the short video offered succinct historical context and the program lineup looked engaging. Rachel smiled until she reached the last paragraph.

> The trail to *Terrain and Town* was a treacherous one, corresponding to the rugged countryside depicted in some of the landscapes. Originally scheduled to open a year ago, the exhibition was derailed by *Monet's Moments: Impressionist Paintings*, a mediocre travelling show. Perhaps this led to a cooling of relations with the Ramsay family, as they unaccountably delayed the shipment of their works to the gallery, a matter on which TAG's administration declined to comment. When such discerning collectors exceed their generosity as lenders by also donating money to support the exhibition and programs, it seems foolhardy to upset them, especially at this crucial time for TAG. With its recent launch of a fundraising campaign for the new wing, in an extraordinary manner as reported in this paper, the gallery needs philanthropic allies. The Ramsays have apparently decided to accept that role, and it remains to be seen if other patrons will follow suit. *Terrain and Town* may well persuade them that TAG deserves their backing.

Rachel felt that senior managers would not like that dredging-up of TAG internal problems, but she felt gratified by the positive mention of her department. Then the day's work took over until she met Tina at six in Littlewood Court.

"Cheers," said Tina. "I bet you're glad you've reached this night." They clinked glasses, their first time doing so since their evening at Buzz's. Rachel looked around the Court. Not as highly decorated as it had been four weeks ago for the gala, it still summoned up a special occasion, with flowers adorning the low stage, scattered highboy cocktail tables covered in stretchy white fabric, two cash bars on opposite sides, and wait staff starting to circulate with appetizer-laden trays. Some members had headed straight upstairs for a quick look at the *Terrain and Town* exhibition and others chose to chat over a drink while waiting for the speeches. She and Tina stood in one of the arches surrounding the Court, where they could survey the crowd.

"Yeah. I won't say that I missed Jeremy, but I did realize just how much he contributed to an exhibition. Helping with that video production took a lot of time, on top of everything else."

"What about education's budget? It must have been fun to deal with that as well."

"It took ages to sort out that deficit, but I think I did it. Like I said, over-spending on the summit and travel and interpretive planning. I can't see that any other areas have contributed to it."

"There's your culprit," said Tina, looking to their left. Rachel followed her glance to see a young woman taking what looked like a business card from Jeremy. As if on cue, he headed over to them.

"Hello Rachel, Tina," he said, smiling at each of them. Rachel looked in disbelief at her old nemesis. Jeremy appeared as self-assured as ever, unfazed by his eviction from the gallery. She noticed that his eyes weren't flicking around in search of more important people; rather, his air conveyed their good fortune at having his attention. He beamed as the gallery photographer popped up and urged the three of them to look his way. Then he held out a business card to Rachel. "You might be needing my help." She took it and read, "Jeremy Singer. Museum Consultant. Specialist in Visitor Engagement."

She looked at him, struggling to keep her expression neutral. Jeremy's frequent presentations at workshops and conferences, extolling the virtues of visitor engagement, had generated a quasi-cult among educators, who eagerly adopted his words to help persuade their bosses of their program ideas. She didn't know if she could ever inspire such hero-worship, but she certainly did not feel the need for his consultancy skills. She would love to tell him to buzz off, but settled for, "You've set up your own business?"

"Yes, I think there's a real need for such freelance work," he said, ignoring the skeptical expression on Tina's face. "I'm sure you're going to have more than you can handle with all the interpretive planning that I started. I'll make sure the new head of education knows about me too."

Tina's expression changed to innocent as she said, "Jeremy, you don't have to worry about your legacy here. Your email etiquette inspires us all." Ignoring his alarmed look, she went on, "Rachel's actually done well picking up after your unfortunate departure. You'll see that when you go through the exhibition."

Jeremy's face tightened as he nodded at Rachel. "You've got my card," he said.

As he left the Court, the two women stared at each other for a moment, then Tina laughed.

"I'll say one thing for Stinger, he's got nerve," she said. "'You might be needing my help.' Give me a break."

At that moment Nick arrived, kissed Rachel, and asked why they were smiling. Rachel explained their enlightening chat with Jeremy, while Tina dove into the crowd to find her husband. Nick took the card from her and read, "Specialist in Visitor Engagement."

He looked up with a grin. "I guess the card's too small to add 'and Colleague Enragement'."

Rachel quickly swallowed some wine before laughing. Trust Nick to puncture Jeremy's new title. "That's his hidden talent."

"I wonder if he'd recommend naturist tours at other museums. Are you going to have more of them when you become head?"

"Well, I'm not head yet, so we're jumping the gun a bit. Although I just heard that senior management finally wants to confirm a permanent head. I'll find out more on Monday." Rachel paused as Nick smiled. "But you know, naturists have as much right to visit the gallery as anyone else. I think I'd be better at scheduling them at an appropriate time."

"You know," said Nick, holding up the card, "I think you should take advantage of Stinger's offer to help you. Hire him on contract to do specialized tours. Let him do the naturist ones. Au naturel."

Rachel laughed again. "That might result in visitor estrangement."

"Good one. Seriously," said Nick, "He needs *you* now."

"Well, I'm not head yet, as I keep saying. But I must admit my attitude's changed. Just a month ago, I was so eager to leave, but I'm glad I've had the chance to run the department while the others took so long to decide. I think I've shown I can do the work."

"And now you've got a great job offer to consider," he said, lowering his voice in deference to their surroundings. "I know that whatever you do, you'll get to keep your clothes on, but now I'd say you have skin in the game."

Rachel groaned. "You'd better get a drink before the speeches start."

"Good idea," he said with a smile, heading for the bar.

As she watched him go, Rachel thought that she had already made her decision. TAG needed her. It wouldn't be easy, but she felt she could face whatever lay ahead with Nick at her side, as long as his puns didn't lead to spousal derangement.

CHAPTER 30
ARTHUR

The conversational buzz in the Court lowered as expectant faces looked toward the stage. Victor approached the podium to start the remarks.

"Good evening, everybody, and welcome to the opening of *Tureen and Town: The Ramsay Canadian Collection.* I'm Victor Drake, chairman of the board and I'll turn things over to George Caldwell, the director, now."

Tureen and Town! It's not a show of bloody soup pots, thought Arthur. But even the chairman's clumsy gaffe could not ruin his excitement tonight. He moved his hand up to sweep some hair off his forehead, then remembered he'd had a haircut. That and his new suit indicated Barbara's influence: She wanted him to shine at his long-awaited opening.

George emphasized the correct title as he thanked the Ramsays for their loan of the works and financial support of the exhibition and programs, acknowledged staff, especially the exhibitions department, and promoted the TAG21 campaign. Then Arthur spoke, thanking the Ramsays and his colleagues, briefly describing the collection, and conveying his gratification at finally bringing it to the public.

"I hope you all enjoy the exhibition." Arthur gathered his notes and turned toward his seat, while George arose for concluding remarks. He stopped in surprise as Alex Ramsay strode to the podium. The gallery photographer, who had started to melt into the crowd, pushed his way back to the edge of the stage.

"I know this is unplanned," said Alex, "but I beg a few moments to say something important." He half turned toward George and Arthur, who sat down, looking concerned. "I'm Alex Ramsay. My parents built this beautiful collection over a long time, and I'd like to thank them for their commitment to Canadian art." He led the applause. "We've all been very pleased to work with Art Matlock, an old family friend, over many years in bringing the show to you. He's done a terrific job and we're so proud to see our paintings, watercolours, and drawings displayed so beautifully. Thanks, Art." He turned toward Arthur as more applause welled up. Arthur smiled and nodded, wondering what Alex was leading up to, as the other Ramsays turned toward him and clapped.

"On behalf of my parents, my wife, and my sister, I have chosen this moment to make an announcement. We know that the Toronto Art Gallery is embarking on an ambitious fundraising campaign for a new wing and other improvements." Arthur noticed that George sat up and looked more interested. "We would like to be a part of that project. We will donate one million dollars to the campaign."

Applause rose again, members looked at each other in surprise, and George leaped toward the podium. Before he could grab the microphone, Alex stood his ground, waited for silence, and said, "We stipulate that this amount go toward the refurbishments planned for the Canadian historical area." George's smile faded for a moment, then returned, as he clapped enthusiastically. Arthur felt stunned.

"One last thing," said Alex, glancing at George who stood beside him at the podium, barely hiding his eagerness to regain the microphone. "My mother's not fond of public speaking so she asked me to say this. She's very impressed, as we all are, by the work carried out by the education and public programs department here. We like the material produced for our exhibition and we know they have planned some wonderful engaging programs to take place over the next few months. So, in addition to our campaign donation, we're very pleased to donate one hundred thousand dollars to this department." Arthur heard a small yelp from the left side of the Court and saw Rachel clap her hands on her mouth while her husband hugged her.

George swerved in front of Alex, thanked him, and encouraged everyone to visit the exhibition. Arthur, astonished by the news, found himself surrounded by Ramsays as a waiter arrived with a tray of wine. Then he noticed the director and Canadian curator from the National Gallery approach the stage. Arthur clinked his glass once more, then courteously disentangled himself to head toward the visitors with Barbara. George homed in as well, trailing Victor behind him.

After introductions, the two men lavished praise on *Terrain and Town*.

"Wonderful show. Beautifully installed. Congratulations on beating us to this one," said the director.

The curator added, "I agree. And it offers new scholarship on Canadian art. Fantastic coup."

"We're very proud of Arthur for bringing us this fabulous exhibition," said George, startling Arthur as he clapped him on the back. "The Canadian collection is the heart of the gallery." Arthur caught a skeptical look on Barbara's face and a miffed expression on Victor's, both ignored by George. "The show's already travelling to a few places. Maybe you'd have room for it in a year or so?" At the director's eager, "It's possible," George ushered the two men a few feet away, nodding to Arthur and Victor as he did so and waving over the gallery photographer.

Arthur noticed that Victor looked a bit forlorn as George moved away with the National Gallery officials. But the chairman rallied enough to say, "Congratulations, Arthur. Great show." They shook hands quickly before Victor's wife whisked him away to someone who wanted to know how many horses he owned. *First time Victor's ever noticed me*, Arthur thought. He sipped his wine, watching George and the two men in animated conversation. It was also the first time he had ever seen George so excited about his department. As Barbara slipped her arm through his, he thought again how this exhibition was yielding all sorts of unexpected pleasures.

Once the delivery was rescheduled, Barbara had turned into an ally for Arthur. She kept attending yoga sessions, but chose times when Damian's assistant led the class. When some naturists complained that they'd heard that the late-night news showed the projection of them on the staircase, Barbara assured them that for the few seconds it appeared, nobody was recognizable. She persuaded the two litigious members to drop their lawsuit against the gallery, convincing them the cameraman had deleted the brief recording of their appearance in the hallway. Arthur learned of the cancelled lawsuit at another dinner with Barbara, after which he enjoyed seeing her naked again, this time in a more romantic setting than his beloved Canadian galleries. Touching allowed. No Damian around to disrupt the action.

"Do you think your parents could stand to live without their paintings for a few more months?" he asked, nodding toward George's group.

"That director doesn't sound like he thinks they're dingy, so maybe," Barbara answered. "I'm sure they'd love to see them hanging at the National Gallery."

"You seem to be much closer to Margaret and Alastair than you used to be. How much did you have to do with the surprise Alex sprung tonight?"

"Even after we went ahead with the delivery of the paintings, I was still pissed off at that Caldwell. How dare he insult us, and you, like that. I thought, well, if all he wants is money, let's give some, but for you. I'm so interested in how you want to refurbish your galleries." Barbara smiled at him as she squeezed his arm. *God you've got beautiful eyes*, thought Arthur, as he fixated on them. Then they moved away from his.

"Oh, hello Damian."

Arthur's heart sank as he turned to see Damian, looking impossibly cool in a black linen suit and white shirt open to mid-chest, lean in to peck Barbara's cheek. A young woman with long, curly hair stood beside him.

"Hi Barbara, Arthur," said Damian.

"I didn't know you were such an art-lover," said Arthur, without thinking. He immediately regretted his snarky tone, but Damian seemed oblivious.

"Sure. This place has some great spaces for yoga," he replied. "Naomi here's just been telling me about her cool family programs. She'd love to offer yoga classes. Get everyone feeling mellow around art."

"Great idea," said Barbara. "I've realized that's possible even when you keep your clothes on." *Don't encourage him*, thought Arthur.

"I hope you won't forget us naturists, Barbara," said Damian, glancing at her arm entwined with Arthur's. "Come on, Naomi, show me this family space you were telling me about."

"How could I forget you, Damian?" Barbara said as the other two walked away. Arthur turned to her, concerned, then relaxed as she smiled. "He brought us together."

As an elderly man, a long-time member, approached to congratulate Arthur on *Terrain and Town*, Barbara withdrew her arm from his and said, "I see the girls over there." She waved at her daughter and Arthur's niece. "I'll take them to the exhibition while you mingle. It's a big night for you. We'll celebrate later." With a pat on his arm, she flowed into the crowd, leaving Arthur neglecting the patron for a moment as he watched her and contemplated what "celebrate" meant. The "treacherous trail" bringing *Terrain and Town* to fruition was now levelling out. Smiling, he bent to listen to the man's question.

CHAPTER 31
AMANDA

Amanda, eager to escape the Ramsay opening as soon as she decently could, paid little attention to the speeches, although she noticed several moments of extra clapping and excited reactions on the stage and in the crowd. She had already courted high-end patrons and donors at last Wednesday's Gold Leaf Circle preview. It was far more conducive to her networking than a mere members' opening, but she dutifully showed up, as Roger expected her to. When she finished her wine, she would leave.

She caught sight of Justin in the crowd, once again sporting his Support Canadian Artists Now T-shirt. *Always a good slogan*, she thought, but not as necessary for her as it had been a month ago. Things had fallen into place for the contemporary department once development informed her and George of Steven's donation. George had unaccountably asked her how her search for a patron for the sculpture commission was going, and he dropped all mention of Zach Drake and embarrassing security tapes. She had heard in a curatorial meeting that things were proceeding smoothly with the appraisal process for the Drake donation, so she assumed that the dubious Lionel Hathaway must be out of the picture. At the Gold Leaf Circle reception, she had introduced George to the Steinbergs, the couple who wanted to fund the sculpture commission, who fortunately had not attended the gala. The media release announcing this news had gone out today. She sipped her wine. She was back in charge!

Most of the throng headed upstairs to view *Terrain and Town*, while others, mainly gallery staff, lined up at the bars. Now that the stage had cleared, a pianist began tinkling the keys, which encouraged a laid-back ambience in the Court. Amanda glanced over at George, wondering who he was talking to, then saw Simon Kinsella approach her.

"Hi Amanda. You must be happy. I saw an interesting media release today." As he adjusted his glasses, Amanda couldn't help thinking of an eager puppy, sniffing at the prospect of a treat.

"Simon, hello. Yes. It's a thrilling announcement for us. The Steinbergs are big supporters of contemporary art. I can't wait to get started on the project."

"It's taken quite a shift from the first announcement," persisted Simon, looking at her closely. "I assume Reid's no longer a candidate. Did the Parkdale Artists Collective have anything to do with that decision?" They both looked over at Justin, whose companions looked as if they had the same T-shirt at home, even if they weren't wearing it now.

"The gallery believes in paying attention to the community," said Amanda. She had just recognized who George was talking to. "Simon, I must go, but why don't we meet soon? Call my secretary to make an appointment."

"Sure. Maybe you'll tell me who you're going to choose for the commission," said Simon hopefully. Amanda finished her wine, smiled, and plunked the empty glass on a table. She had to detach the National Gallery's director and curator from George's grip. They may have come to see the Ramsay show, but she would make sure they saw the Havilio installation too. After all, she had beaten them to it. She made a beeline toward them.

CHAPTER 32
GEORGE

As Amanda sauntered away with the two National Gallery men, George turned to face Victor, who gave him a calculating look and asked, "The Ramsays have coughed up. What does that bring us up to?"

"Fifty-nine million. One million short of our goal a month ago, but still good news," said George, extending his glass to clink with Victor's.

"Especially after what that hack wrote today. Good thing my interviews are coming out soon, to give this place some decent coverage."

"Kinsella's article was mostly positive, Victor," said George, quelling his irritation. He knew that Victor had had a hard time over the past few weeks, adjusting to media coverage of Zach's failing business and to TAG's protocols regarding his donation's tax benefit. The chairman had not followed through on his threat to discuss George's job prospects with the board. Time to offer a sop to Victor's ego. "And your interviews will do a lot for the new wing."

"Hmmph. Of course they will. Good thing there's no ruckus tonight. No kids, no nudists, no protesting artists. You've got your gallery under control for once."

George didn't miss a beat, accustomed by now to the pronoun dance.

"Let's concentrate on the good news tonight. I think it augurs well for our campaign. You're doing a fantastic job representing our gallery" —

except when you screw up the titles of exhibitions — "and I'm sure there are some likely donors here tonight. Shall we go up to the exhibition?"

Victor nodded and looked around for his wife. As the couple headed upstairs, George held back. He scanned the Court to see if there was anyone he should speak to here. There was Arthur, looking the happiest that George had ever seen him, chatting to a few older members. He wondered if that Barbara Ramsay had anything to do with Arthur's good cheer, as he had noticed them arm in arm earlier. In another corner, that damn Kinsella looked pretty chummy with Justin. *Our very own artists' rights activist*, thought George bitterly. No doubt feeding Kinsella some lines about supporting Canadian artists for his next article. He'd let Amanda handle the response to that if it threw any mud on TAG. The commission was all hers now.

George wondered if the current good mood of two of his curators would help the campaign grow. At that moment the chief curator sidled up to him, looking pleased.

"George, I have some good news. Maybe development has already told you, but at the Gold Leaf Circle night, the Haddads promised one million," said Roger.

"Super! They were at the gala, weren't they? How did you get them to change their minds?"

"They weren't all that upset, just bemused. When I assured them that we prefer our gallery nudes on canvas rather than in the flesh, they came around." Roger's eyes twinkled.

George's lips twitched into a sardonic smile. "I should have known we weren't done with the jokes from that night." He slapped Roger's shoulder. "Well done. Let's hope the rest of the campaign proceeds better than its launch." As if warning that that might be easier said than done, the pianist swung into "Pennies from Heaven."

Roger nodded and shrugged. George started ascending the grand staircase. As he reached the landing, he stopped for a moment and involuntarily checked that Miss Littlewood's bust was fastened securely. He knew it had been re-bolted after that fateful night, but his faith in his staff had dipped somewhat. He glanced up at the discreetly positioned camera, part of the ongoing *Gestes* exhibition.

All four were left on for tonight, as the whole gallery, not just the Ramsay show, was open for the members' enjoyment. He rarely stopped to look at the bust. *So any viewers outside have a rare treat now*, he thought wryly. Founder and Director. From SLAG to TAG. TAG21. George still thought that the campaign's title conveyed the right message to lure the required contributions for his vision. In fact, he was shocked that the fundraising had flourished so well, after the debacle four weeks ago.

"Sorry, old girl," he whispered to Miss Littlewood's serene likeness. "We won't let that happen again. Onward and upward." His gaze lingered. The sculpture appeared to emit an aura he'd never seen before, as if offering silent encouragement. Then chatter above reminded him that there were still potential donors to cajole, and he started climbing the stairs. He wouldn't interfere with their enjoyment of *Gestes*, but he could encourage them to look at the model in the lobby and consider donating to the campaign. Feeling more like the master of his domain than he had in awhile, in spite of another knee twinge, George girded himself anew for this never-ending task. He reached the top of the stairs and walked briskly down the hallway.

ACKNOWLEDGEMENTS

I'm grateful to my first readers, Jane Austin, Diana Brooks, Ingrid Kolt, Frank Sullivan, and Kate Sullivan, whose responses helped me to persevere. My mentors in the Vancouver Manuscript Intensive challenged me in ways that were daunting but necessary. Thanks to Sally Gregson and Bridget Chandler, who were always ready to share comments about writing. On the long route to publication, *In the Frame* crossed paths for a time with The Porcupine's Quill, and I'm grateful to Stephanie Small for her love of satire and rigorous notes. While I only read small sections of this book at meetings of the West End Writers, I've appreciated the support offered by this group. Many thanks to Greg Ioannou, Cheryl Hawley, Amanda Feeney, and Jonathan Relph at Iguana Books for bringing this novel into the world. To my friends who expressed eagerness to read *In the Frame*: that spurred me on more than I can say. I hope your patience is rewarded with a few laughs.

ABOUT THE AUTHOR

Pat Sullivan built her career as an educator at the Art Gallery of Ontario, Toronto, and at the Agnes Etherington Art Centre, Kingston, Ontario. *In the Frame* is her first novel. Pat lives in Vancouver, British Columbia.

www.patriciasullivan.ca